1天10分鐘，
英語和人生都起飛

抄寫英語
的奇蹟

Brett Lindsay
林熙——著

THE MIRACLE
OF TRANSCRIBING ENGLISH
10 Minutes a Day
to Skyrocket Your English and Life

前言
每天 10 分鐘，完全改造你的英文和人生

　　歡迎踏上掌握英文與豐潤人生的旅程。我是林熙 Brett Lindsay，作為 SAT 面授老師與線上英文老師，我不僅教授與課程相關的內容，也培養學生積極的學習態度。具體來說，我幫助他們在遇到挫折與挑戰時調適心態、改變方法。這二十五年來指導了許多學生，而我的目標是幫助更多的人，實現他們想要的生活與出色的英文能力。因此，我為你帶來了這本書，在提升你的語言能力同時，也提供見解帶你走向充實的人生。在內文中，你將看到 100 篇鼓舞人心的文章集結，每一篇就像盞明燈，指引你走過 10 個人生重要的主題：感恩、克服逆境、學習、目標與夢想、愛、恆毅力、快樂、成長、自我關懷、人生觀。

　　能夠提升英文能力並擁有更好人生的絕佳方法是什麼？我提出簡單又有奇效的方法：每天花 10-15 分鐘閱讀這本書的一篇文章，並持續 100 天。但不要只是閱讀，而是沉浸在這些想法裡，抄寫它們或唸出來。讓這些智慧滲透到你的日常生活中，見證你的英文能力和個人發展的成長。

　　抄寫是一個強大的學習工具，透過多種感官啟動與高強度積極參與，來提升你的英文學習體驗。不同於主要只有使用視覺並經常造成快速遺忘的被動式閱讀，抄寫文本要求你高度關注每個單字、拼字、句子結構和文法。這種涉及視覺、聽覺和觸覺的積極參與，不但提高你的寫作技能，深化你對英文細微差別的理解，還有助於你將字彙、文法與觀念牢記在腦海中。透過抄寫投入額外的努力和時間，你更有可能做到內化這些文章的教導與智慧，並能夠將它們有意義地應用於你的人生中。記住，有效的學習需要較慢的方法：深入學習文本，可以確保你記得更持久與擁有影響深遠的理解。

　　你可能會想知道，為什麼不將同個主題的文章放在一起？答案在於我們大腦運轉的方式。學習在動態、多變時，最為有效。間隔重複，是每間隔一段時間再次接觸類似主題的方法，不僅加深印象，同時會將新學到的內容與腦裡已有的東西產生連結，有效鞏固與擴大記憶量。本書的架構就是利用了這種學習

技巧，確保每天帶來一個新主題、新視角。

　　這本書適合所有人，無論年齡或職業。無論你是高中生、職場專業人士，還是享受退休生活的人，這些文章都會引起你的共鳴。使用日常英文撰寫，語言難度對於已有高中英文程度的讀者來說是好懂的，並且提供中文譯文有助於理解。此外，這本書對於正處在人生每個階段的人來說，是一份美好的禮物，充滿智慧。

　　與這本書互動的兩種主要方法：抄寫和唸出來。在下一節「如何充分利用本書」中將有詳細討論，不僅可以增強你的英文技能，還可以加深你對每篇文章所傳達的人生課程的理解。

　　當你踏上這趟旅程時，我鼓勵你擁抱其中的想法，讓它們啟發並挑戰你。如果你這樣做，我相信不僅你的英文能力會有所提高，你的人生與你周遭的一切也會產生積極的改變。

　　祝你在這次啟發的旅程中一切順利！

林熙 Brett Lindsay

Preface
10 minutes a day can totally transform your English and life

Welcome to a journey that combines the mastery of the English language with the enrichment of life itself. I am Brett Lindsay, and as an in-person SAT teacher and online English teacher, I teach not only the content related to the courses but also establish a positive learning attitude in my students. Specifically, I help them adjust their mindset and change their methods when facing setbacks and challenges. Having guided many students for twenty-five years, I aim to help more people achieve the life they desire and excellent English proficiency. Therefore, I bring to you a book designed not just to enhance your linguistic skills but also to offer insights into leading a fulfilling life. In these pages, you will discover a collection of 100 inspirational articles, each a beacon guiding you through 10 significant themes: gratitude, conquering adversity, learning, goals & dreams, love, grit, happiness, growth, self-care, and philosophy.

What is the best way to both improve your English and lead a better life? I propose a simple yet powerful approach: spend 10-15 minutes each day for 100 days reading an article from this book. But don't just read; immerse yourself in the ideas, transcribe them, or read them out loud. Let the wisdom seep into your daily life and witness the transformation in both your command of English and your personal development.

Transcription is a powerful learning tool that elevates your English learning experience by engaging multiple senses and demanding active participation. Unlike passive reading, which primarily uses your sense of sight and often leads to quick forgetting, transcribing a text requires you to focus intensely on each word, its spelling, sentence structure, and grammar. This active engagement, which involves sight, hearing, and touch, not only enhances your writing skills and deepens your understanding of English nuances but also helps to fix vocabulary, grammar, and ideas firmly in your mind. By investing this extra effort and time in transcription, you are more likely to internalize the lessons and wisdom of the text, allowing you to apply them meaningfully to your life. Remember, effective learning requires a slower approach: engaging deeply with the material ensures a more lasting and impactful understanding.

You might wonder, why not group similar themes together? The answer lies in the way our brains are wired. Learning is most effective when it is dynamic and varied. Spaced repetition is a method where similar topics are revisited after intervals of time. This not only deepens the impression but also connects newly learned content with existing knowledge in the brain, effectively solidifying and expanding memory capacity. This book is structured to leverage this technique, ensuring each day brings a new theme, a fresh perspective.

This book is for everyone, regardless of age or career. Whether you're a high school student, a working professional, or enjoying retirement, these articles will resonate with you. Crafted in everyday English, the language is accessible to people with a senior high school level of proficiency, and the translations provided will aid in understanding. Moreover, this book serves as an ideal gift, brimming with wisdom for individuals at every stage of life.

There are two main methods to engage with the text: transcribing and reading aloud. Each method, thoroughly discussed in the next section, "How to get the most out of this book," will not only bolster your English skills but also deepen your understanding of the life lessons each article imparts.

As you embark on this journey, I encourage you to embrace the ideas within. Let them inspire and challenge you. If you do, I am confident that not only will your English improve, but you'll also bring positive changes to your life and to those around you.

Wishing you all the best on this enlightening journey!

Brett Lindsay

目次 CONTENTS

Phase 1
Embark on Journey of Change 踏上改變

Phase 2
Establish Objectives 確立目標

Phase 3
Launch Action Steps 展開行動

Phase 4
Gradually Advance 逐步前進

Phase 5
Persistently Execute 堅持執行

Phase 6
Integrate into Life 融入生活

Phase 7
Embrace Results 迎接成果

Phase 8
Reflect on Outcomes 回顧反思

Phase 9
Consolidate and Stabilize 鞏固穩定

如何充分利用本書

💗 英文母語人士口說和寫作的自然風格

　　這本書我選擇用非正式的口語英文編寫，來反映出母語人士在日常情境中的溝通方式（除了在非常正式的學術場合外）。這是我深思熟慮後的選擇，因為在現實生活中，母語人士在口說和寫作時大多是用非正式的英文。藉由擁抱這種風格，你會發現自己的英文更接近母語人士講述和書寫的自然風格。

💗 與文本互動

　　想透過本書獲得最極致的受益，需要主動地使用多種感官與文本互動。好的學習是用正確的練習來養成積極的習慣。當你在閱讀文章時，應該致力於內化良好的發音，你可以聆聽我錄製的文章音檔（掃描書上 QR 碼獲取音檔）來增強這個技能。這種邊聽邊讀的過程，可以確保你下意識地採用母語人士的發音。你可以用多種方式與音檔互動：被動聆聽以習慣發音、語調和節奏；同步聆聽和默讀；逐句跟讀（播放一個句子，按暫停，唸出句子）；同步跟著音檔，唸出來。順道一提，我至今仍然使用這個絕妙的方法來練習中文。

　　一旦你牢牢記住了我的聲音，你就應該開口唸出文章，並開始進行一字不漏的抄寫。用鉛筆寫下文本，回想著音檔的聲音，單字的發音、句子的語調以及整個段落的節奏。一邊唸一邊寫，來深入鞏固你的英文學習成果。你應該這樣做幾次？至少五次，多多益善。對了，如果英文文本中有你看不懂的地方，可以參考中文譯文來幫助你理解整篇文章。記住，你在這些段落上投入的時間和感官的參與越多，學習就會越有成效。

💗 融入你的生活

　　理想的作法是每天在特定時間使用這本書，像是剛起床或是睡覺前。持之以恆是關鍵，如果有一天太忙，至少聆聽和唸出來這一天的文章。這樣可以維持你的習慣並保持學習過程的活躍。

　　許多文章有你可以行動的環節，從簡單到需要更多的投入。我也介紹了一些可以輕鬆融入你日常生活的習慣，不僅提高你的英文能力，也豐富了你的人生。

 成長之旅

　　這本書不只是一個學語言的工具，它也是你走過人生各階段和挑戰的伙伴。隨著你的成長，記得保持開放的心態，並根據你的需求來調整練習。你的目標是在 100 天內不間斷地完成這本書，之後你可以隨時多次回顧和探索它。

　　在這 100 天結束時，你會發現不只是你的英文，還有你對人生的看法也會受益匪淺。為你一天天的學習與成長之旅，舉杯！

掃描 QR Code，
即可聆聽音檔

How to Use This Book

🤍 The Natural Style of Speaking and Writing of Native English Speakers

This book is written in an informal, conversational English that mirrors how native speakers communicate in everyday scenarios, except for very formal academic settings. This choice is deliberate, as real-life English is mostly informal, both in speech and writing. By embracing this style, you'll find yourself closer to the natural style of English as it is spoken and written by native speakers.

🤍 Engaging with the Text

Maximizing the benefits from this book requires active engagement with the texts, using multiple senses. Good learning involves practicing correctly to develop positive habits. As you read, aim to internalize good pronunciation, a skill you can enhance by listening to my recordings of the passages (accessible via QR code). This process of listening while reading ensures that you subconsciously adopt native-speaker pronunciation. You can engage with the audio in various ways: passive listening for pronunciation, intonation, and rhythm; simultaneously listening and reading silently; play and pause listening (play a sentence, pause, and read the sentence out loud); or reading aloud following the audio. Btw, I still use this fantastic method to practice Chinese.

Once you've got my voice firmly in your mind, you should read the text aloud and write it down, word for word. Write down the text with a pencil, recalling the sound of the audio recording (the pronunciation of the words, the intonation of the sentences, and the rhythm of the entire passage). Read aloud and write simultaneously to deeply consolidate the results of your English learning. How many times should you do this? At least five times, the more the better. By the way, if there are parts of the English text you don't understand, you can refer to the Chinese translation to help you understand the overall article. Remember: the more time and sensory engagement you invest in these passages, the more effective your learning will be.

♥ Fitting It into Your Life

The ideal approach is to dedicate a specific time each day to this book, either just after waking up or before going to bed. Consistency is key. If a day gets too busy, at least listen to and read the article out loud. This maintains your habit and keeps the learning process active.

Many articles include actionable steps, ranging from the simple to those requiring more dedication. Some introduce habits that can be easily integrated into your daily routine, not only enhancing your English but also enriching your life.

♥ A Journey of Growth

This book isn't just a tool to learn language; it's a companion on your journey through life's various stages and challenges. As you progress, remember to keep an open mind and adapt the exercises to suit your needs. Your goal is to complete the book in 100 days, without stopping. Afterward, you can always revisit and explore it multiple times. By the end of these 100 days, you'll find not only your English, but also your perspective on life, profoundly enriched. Here's to a journey of learning and growth, one day at a time.

Phase
1

. . . .

Embark on Journey
of Change

踏上改變

"When you start appreciating what you have,
instead of lamenting what you don't have,
something shifts."

-from Day 1-

「當你開始感激自己所擁有的東西，
而不是哀嘆自己所沒有的東西時，
有些事就會改變。」

Gratitude 感恩

The Secret to Feeling Rich.

Gratitude is like a magical lens that changes how you see things. When you start appreciating what you have, instead of lamenting what you don't have, something shifts. It's like suddenly, what you have multiplies in value. It's not about having a lot—it's about appreciating what you have. That's the secret to feeling truly rich. So, even on tough days, finding something, no matter how small, to be thankful for, can change the way you view life. It's about realizing that even the simplest things can bring joy, and in recognizing that, you find contentment. It's really an awesome way to live.

感到富有的祕訣

感恩就像一個神奇的鏡片，可以改變你看待事物的方式。當你開始感激自己所擁有的東西，而不是哀嘆自己所沒有的東西時，有些事就會改變。就像突然之間，你所擁有的事物價值倍增。重要的不是你擁有很多，而是珍惜你所擁有的。這就是真正感到富有的祕訣。因此，即使在艱難的日子裡，你也要找到一些值得感激的事情，無論是多麼小的事情，都可以改變你看待人生的方式。這意思是說：意識到最簡單的事情也能帶來快樂，並且真正發覺到它，你會發現自己感到知足，這確實是一種很棒的生活方式。

lament 哀嘆　shift 轉變　multiply 倍增、加倍
realize 發覺、意識到　contentment 知足、滿足

Conquering Adversity 克服逆境

Laugh Away Life's Burdens.

You ever notice how sometimes life seems too heavy? Next time you're in a funk, try this—just laugh. Go watch something funny, such as a movie or sitcom, or hang out with that friend who cracks you up. You know why? Laughter's like this magical stress buster. When you laugh, your brain releases these feel-good chemicals, and suddenly the weight on your shoulders feels lighter. I'm not saying laughter's going to solve all your problems, but it's gonna make them a whole lot easier to tackle. So, go ahead, give yourself a break and let loose a few laughs. You'll feel more relaxed, and who knows, the answer you've been looking for might just pop into your head.

一笑解千愁

你有沒有注意到有時生活似乎太沉重了？下次當你鬱悶消沉時，試試這個——笑一笑。去看一些好笑的東西，像是電影、喜劇影集等，或者和那個會讓你哈哈大笑的朋友一起出去。你知道為什麼嗎？笑就像個神奇的壓力消除器。當你笑的時候，你的大腦會釋放讓人感覺良好的化學物質，突然間你會感覺到肩膀上的重量輕了許多。我並不是說笑能解決你所有的問題，但它會讓問題整個變得更容易處理。所以，開始做吧，讓自己休息一下，放聲大笑。你會覺得放鬆許多，而且誰知道呢，說不定你一直在尋找的答案突然就會在你腦中靈光乍現。

funk 鬱悶、消沉　sitcom 喜劇影集
stress buster 壓力消除器　release 分泌、釋放

Learning 學習

Practice Doesn't Necessarily Make Perfect!

Does "practice make perfect?" Not quite! Practice makes permanent, but only perfect practice makes perfect. Keep that in mind when you're honing your skills. Don't fall into the trap of mindless repetition, as that might just reinforce bad habits. Make sure you're always fully engaged and mindful in your practice, aiming for improvement each time. And hey, this rule applies to copying texts from this book as well! Focus on your actions and work toward excellence. That way, you'll not only improve but also build a strong foundation for future success. Always remember, the quality of your practice is just as important, if not more, than the quantity.

熟練不一定能生巧

「熟就一定能生巧嗎？」不見得！其實練習會養成永久的慣性，然而只有完美的練習才能真正讓成果達到完美。記得，當你在練習技能時，不要掉進無腦重複的陷阱裡，因為這可能只是在加深你不好的習慣。確保你在練習時總是全神貫注、專心致志，並以每次練習都要進步為目標。對了，這個規則也適用在你抄寫這本書的時候！專注於你的執行，努力追求卓越。這樣一來，你不但會進步，還能為未來的成功打好堅實的基礎。永遠要記住，練習的品質與次數一樣重要，甚至還要重要。

permanent 永久的　trap 陷阱　hone 練習
reinforce 加強、加深　fully engaged 全神貫注的

Day 4

Goals & Dreams 目標與夢想

The Definition of Insanity.

Albert Einstein once said, "The definition of insanity is doing the same thing over and over again and expecting different results." When you've been doing something for quite a while, such as trying to figure out a math problem, but you're not making any progress, you may have fallen into this trap. The most important thing you can do is to stop what you've been doing and try a different method. Even if the new method doesn't work, it will at least give you a new angle on the problem and may give you a new idea you can use to solve it. Keep changing your approach and eventually, you'll find a method that works. So, remember: if one approach isn't working, take another approach.

精神錯亂的定義

阿爾伯特・愛因斯坦說過：「精神錯亂的定義就是一遍又一遍地做同樣的事情，卻期待有不同的結果。」當你做一件事做了很久，例如一直想解出一道數學題目，卻沒有任何進展，你可能已經陷入了這樣的困境。你能做的最重要的事情就是停止你一直在做的事，並嘗試不同的方法。即使新方法沒有奏效，它至少會給你一個看待問題的新角度，並可能給你一個可以用來解決問題的新想法。不斷改變你的方法，最終你會找到一個有用的方法。所以，請記住：如果一個方法不管用，就請採取另一個方法。

definition 定義　insanity 精神錯亂
angle 角度　approach 方法

Love 愛

Don't Let Your Love Disappear Faster Than an Ice Cream on a Hot Day.

Hey, let's be real. In daily life, it's so easy to forget what made you fall head over heels for your partner in the first place. But here's the deal—really noticing their great qualities is the secret to keeping the love alive. If you let yourself focus on what annoys you, well, you'll see your affection disappear faster than an ice cream on a hot day. So, here's your takeaway: actively appreciating what makes your lover awesome is like a golden ticket to a happier relationship. It's like falling in love over and over again. Do it regularly and you're not just maintaining love, you're increasing that love.

別讓感情消失得比大熱天的冰淇淋還要快

嘿，我們來講真話。在日常生活中，很容易忘了當初是什麼讓你傾心於你的另一半。但事情是這樣的 —— 好好留意他們美好的特質是維持愛情的祕訣。如果你讓自己的焦點放在不滿的地方，那麼，會發現你的感情消失得比大熱天的冰淇淋還要快。所以這是你的收穫：積極地欣賞你最喜歡愛人的什麼地方，這就像一張通往更幸福美好關係的黃金入場券。像是一次又一次地墜入愛河。定期這樣做，你不僅可以維持愛情，還可以注入更多的愛。

partner 伴侶　quality 特質　annoy 使人不滿、煩
affection 感情　takeaway 收穫

Grit 恆毅力

How Do You Eat an Elephant?

There's an old saying, "How do you eat an elephant?", to which the answer is "One bite at a time." Got a big goal? Awesome! Slice it into bite-sized pieces. These little chunks are your milestones. It's much easier for you to believe you can achieve these smaller goals, which gives you more motivation to do the necessary work to achieve them. And here's another key: every time you tick something off your list, give yourself a pat on the back. It could be a treat, a break, or a bounce on a rebounder—whatever gets you pumped. This isn't just about making progress, either: it's about enjoying the journey, you know? On the other hand, why do most people quit? They set huge, unrealistic goals and think, "I'll never achieve them!" So, set small, doable goals, reward yourself, and keep going! Your persistence is going to pay off, step by victorious step!

要怎麼吃掉一頭大象呢？

俗話說：「要怎麼吃掉一頭大象呢？」答案是：「一口一口地吃。」你有一個大目標嗎？太棒了！把它切成你可以應付的小塊，這些小塊就是你的里程碑。你會更確信自己能完成這些較小的目標，這能帶給你更多的動力去做你必須做的事情來達標。還有另一個重點：每當你完成清單上的一件事時，就要給自己一點鼓勵。可以是一個點心、一個休息，或是在彈跳床上跳一跳——任何能讓你開心的事。這不只是為了要有進度，也是要享受過程，懂嗎？另外，為什麼大部分的人會半途而廢？因為他們設定了太大、不切實際的目標，並認為：「我永遠也達不到！」所以，設定小的、做得到的目標，給自己獎勵和一直前進！你的堅持會得到回報，一步一步走向勝利！

chunk 小塊　milestone 里程碑　treat 點心
rebounder 彈跳床　doable 做得到的

Day 7

Happiness 快樂

Started Questioning the Meaning of Life?

Ever get so tired that you start questioning the meaning of life and find everybody irritating? When you're brimming with resentment, hate life, and are constantly venting, you really need to take a break from work or studies and just get some good sleep. Here's how: First, sleep in a cool, dark room. Also, gradually train your circadian rhythm. This means keeping the same sleeping schedule, even on weekends: go to bed at the same time each night and wake up at the same time. Now, here's a toughie: If you must drink coffee or tea, finish drinking it by 2pm so most of the caffeine is out of your system before bed. If you do all of these things, you'll feel so much more energetic and happier you won't believe it. You'll also be able to think more clearly and deal with difficult problems with ease. Just do it!

開始懷疑人生嗎？

你有沒有曾經因為太疲憊而開始懷疑人生的意義，覺得每個人都讓你感到煩躁？當你滿是怨恨、厭惡生活，不斷地釋出負能量時，你真正需要的是暫時放下工作或課業，好好睡一覺。這樣做吧：首先，在一個涼爽、黑暗的房間裡睡覺。還有，逐漸訓練你的生理時鐘。這意思是你要把作息固定下來，即使在週末也要：每晚同一時間上床睡覺，每天同一時間起床。好，有個比較難做到的點：如果你必須喝咖啡或茶，請確保在下午 2 點前喝完，這樣大部分的咖啡因可以在睡前從你的身體裡排出。如果做到上面所有的建議，你會感到更有活力、快樂到你無法相信的程度。你還能夠更清晰地思考，輕鬆應對困難的問題。就這麼做吧！

irritating 煩躁的　brim with 滿是的　resentment 怨恨
vent 釋出負能量　toughie 難做到的點

Growth 成長

Make Intelligent Choices Every Day.

Life's full of not-so-comfy spots. Whether you're stuck doing something or pushing yourself to grow, you're going to feel a bit uncomfortable either way. Now, here's the amazing thing. Not all discomfort is equal. Take discipline, for example. It's like a little nudge every day, a tiny bit of unease that helps you get closer to your dreams. It's like having a small stone in your shoe on a long, rewarding hike. On the other hand, there's failure. It's like falling flat on your face in front of a crowd—ouch, some serious unease that can really hurt. So, it's kinda like choosing between a small, daily stone or a big, painful fall. Discipline is your daily little stone, while failure is that big nasty fall waiting to happen if you're not careful. So, when it comes to feeling uneasy, pick the small nudge of discipline over the big pain of failure. It's your choice every day. Choose smart!

每天都做聰明的選擇

人生充滿了不怎麼舒服的部分。無論你是陷入困境，還是鞭策自己成長，都會覺得不太舒服。現在跟你說件驚奇的事：不是所有的不舒服都是一樣的。以「自律」來說，它就像每天輕輕地推你一把，這一點點的不適讓你離夢想更近。也像是在長途、有意義的健行裡，你的鞋進了一顆小石頭。另一方面，以「失敗」來說，它就像你在眾人面前摔得一敗塗地 —— 唉喲，真的很不舒服，甚至會讓你非常痛。所以，人生有點像在選擇，你要每天的小石頭，還是一次很痛的大跌倒。自律是你每天的小石頭，而失敗就是那個在等著你不小心時，就來了個糟糕的大摔倒。所以，既然都會覺得不舒服，就要選擇自律的小推動，而不是失敗的大痛苦。這是你每天的選擇，所以聰明地選吧！

spot 部分、點　discipline 自律、紀律
unease 不適　pick 選擇、挑選

Self-Care 自我關懷

Plant Seeds of Positivity for Yourself.

Starting and ending your day with positive thoughts is like nourishing your mind. It fills your day with confidence and good energy. It's a simple yet impactful way to remember your worth. Try this: when you wake up and before you sleep, think of good things about yourself. Maybe tell yourself, "I like myself," "I feel terrific," or "I am a great friend and people appreciate me." This habit is like planting seeds of positivity that grow all day. Doing it regularly helps shape a confident and upbeat mindset. The way you talk to yourself really shapes your day. Lift yourself up each morning and night—it makes a big difference in keeping the positivity flowing!

為自己種下正向的種子

用正面的想法來開始和結束你的一天，就像滋養你的心靈一樣，可以讓你的一天充滿自信和活力。這是簡單又有效的方式，來記得你的個人價值。試試這個：當你醒來後和睡覺前，想想自己好的事情。可以對自己說：「我喜歡自己」「我覺得超讚！」，或者「我是一個很棒的朋友，大家都很欣賞我。」這樣的習慣就像是種下正向的種子，整天都在生長。定期地這樣做，可以幫助你塑造自信和樂觀的心態。你跟自己說話的方式真的會影響你的一天。每天早晚都讓自己振作起來——這對保持源源不絕的正能量有很大的幫助！

036

nourish 滋養　impactful 有效的
shape 塑造　upbeat 樂觀的

Philosophy 人生觀

Pay Attention to the Words You Habitually Use.

A word of caution: select your words wisely. There are so many ways to describe something, and each one will alter how you feel about it. For example, if you lose your wallet, you probably won't be too happy about it. Imagine telling your friend, "I'm so angry I could tear somebody to shreds!" That would make you angrier than you originally were. Imagine instead that you said, "I'm a little upset about it." You wouldn't feel as bad, would you? So, use less intense words when things upset you. On the other hand, you can use this technique for positive things, too. If you had some great pasta, you could say, "That penne was out of this world!" You'd feel even better than if you had said, "That penne was pretty good." This holds true for any language you're using, too. Remember, the stronger your language, the stronger you feel. Therefore, you should be very careful with the words you habitually use.

留心你習慣會用的措辭

給你一個提醒：明智地選擇你的措辭。描述一件事情的方式有很多種，而每一種說法都會影響你對這件事的感受。例如你的錢包掉了，你大概不會太高興。想像你告訴朋友：「我氣到想把人碎屍萬段！」這樣的措辭會讓你比原本還要更加生氣。想像一下，如果反而你是說：「我有點不開心。」你感覺就沒有那麼難受，對吧？所以，當有事情讓你不高興時，試著用沒那麼激烈的字眼。另一方面，這個技巧也能用在正面的事情。像是你吃到很美味的義大利麵，你可以說：「這盤斜管麵簡直超乎世界的好吃！」這會讓你感覺比只說「這盤斜管麵很不錯」還要更好。這可以用在你會使用的任何一種語言。記住，你的用詞越強烈，你的感受也會越強烈。因此，你要小心你習慣會用的措辭。

caution 小心、謹慎　alter 影響、改變
intense 激烈的　habitually 習慣地

Phase
2

· · · · · · · · · · · · ·

Establish Objectives

確立目標

"So don't exhaust yourself chasing after perfection;
instead aim for improvement."

-from Day 18-

「所以，不要為了追求完美而疲憊不堪，
而是應該以進步為目標。」

Day 11

Gratitude 感恩

Kickstart the Day with Gratitude.

Here's a cool little trick to start your day off on the right foot. When you're sipping your morning coffee or tea, think of three different things you're thankful for. And try to mix it up every day. It could be as simple as the sun shining, a good book you're reading, or even that new song that gets you pumped. Doing this gets your brain thinking positively and can make the whole day feel brighter. Plus, it's a moment just for you before the day's hustle kicks in. Give it a try, and you might just notice how even the regular days start to feel a bit more special.

用感恩啟動新的一天

有個很好的小技巧，可以讓你用對的方式來開始新的一天。早上悠哉喝咖啡或茶時，想三件你感謝的事情。每天盡量想比較不一樣的事（增加感謝的多樣性）。很簡單，可以是陽光明媚、一本你正在讀的好書，甚至是一首讓你開心興奮的新歌。這樣做能讓你的大腦正向思考，讓你的一整天都變得更加美好。還有，在一天的忙碌開始前，這也是你的專屬時刻。試試看，你可能會發現，即使是平凡的日子也開始變得比較不平凡了。

trick 技巧　sip 小口慢慢喝、啜飲　pumped 開心的、興奮的
hustle 忙碌　kick in 開始

Day 12

Conquering Adversity 克服逆境

Change the Way You Talk to Yourself.

Listen, life throws curveballs, right? So, here's a cool way to deal with tough times: change how you talk to yourself about them. Instead of going, "Ugh, why me?", switch it to, "Okay, what can I learn here?" It sounds simple, but trust me, it's powerful. You go from being a victim to being like a detective, figuring stuff out. You stop feeling stuck and start looking for answers or new ways to do things. It's all about the mindset. So, the next time something tough comes up, don't just complain. Ask yourself how you can grow from it. Makes the challenge kinda exciting, doesn't it?

改變對自己說話的方式

嘿,聽著,人生總會有沒料到的變化,對吧?所以,有一個應對困境的好方法:改變你對自己說這件事的方式。遇到困難時,不要一直去想:「呃,為什麼是我遇到?」要換個方式問自己:「好吧,那我能從這個困難裡學到什麼?」這聽起來很容易,但相信我,這個思維很強大。你從一個受害者變成了一個偵探,弄清楚事情的真相。你不再覺得自己被卡在困境裡,而是跳出困境開始尋找答案或新的方法。這都是心態問題。所以,下次你遇到困境時,不要只是抱怨,而是要問問自己,怎麼從中成長。這樣也讓這個挑戰變得比較令人興奮,對吧?

curveball 曲線球 （代表：不預期的變化）　victim 受害者
detective 偵探　mindset 心態

Day 13

Learning 學習

The Better the Vocabulary, the Higher the Income.

Let's talk about the power of words. Each new word learned correctly opens up opportunities and helps you express yourself better. And here's something interesting—studies have shown that the better your vocabulary is, the higher your income will be. But there's more. When you have a strong vocabulary, you're able to explain your thoughts more clearly and confidently. People subconsciously judge us by the way we speak and write, and a good vocabulary makes a positive impression. So, make it a habit to learn how to correctly use new words daily and use them in your conversations and writing. And what's the best way to do this? It's simple. Use the example sentences in the dictionary as templates and substitute one or two of those words with one or two of your own words. Of course, you need to keep the word you want to master in the new sentence. Also, keep the parts of speech the same. Say your sentence out loud 5 times, and you will have learned the word!

字彙能力越好，收入越高

來聊聊文字的力量吧。正確地學習每個新字彙，能為你帶來機會，幫助你能夠更好地表達自己。而且有個有趣的事實 —— 研究顯示，你的字彙能力越好，你的收入就越高。還有，當你擁有強大的字彙能力時，你可以更清晰、更自信地說明你的想法。人們會下意識地根據我們說話和寫作的方式來評價我們，而好的用字遣詞能讓人留下正面的印象。所以，要養成每天學習如何正確使用新字彙的習慣，並且在你的日常對話與寫作中運用它們。那麼怎麼做是最好的呢？很簡單。用字典裡的例句來當範本，然後用自己已有的字彙來替換其中的一兩個單字。當然，你在新的造句裡需要保留你想要掌握學習的新字彙。還有，要保持詞性相同。開口說出你新造的句子 5 次，這樣你就學會這個單字了！

subconsciously 下意識地　judge 評價、斷定　template 範本
substitute 替換、取代　part of speech 詞性

Day 14

Goals & Dreams 目標與夢想

Don't Just Set Attainment Goals.

Attainment goals are objectives you set to accomplish specific things, such as obtaining a gold TOEIC certificate or increasing your salary at work. These goals are great, and you should set a completion date for them. However, in some cases, you should not set attainment goals. Instead, you should set action goals, which are goals about how much time you should spend doing something. Let's use reading an English novel as an example. While this is one of the best ways to improve your English, it is usually a mistake to set the goal of reading a certain number of chapters every day or finishing the novel in a certain number of months. That will only stress you out, and you could easily give up. Rather, set an action goal: decide to read the novel a certain number of minutes each day and don't worry about how many pages you read. Remain flexible with your goal, too. You may need to decrease the time on some days, and you may want to increase it on others. Do this, and in a few months, you'll be amazed by how much you've achieved!

不要只有設定成就目標

成就目標是你設定要達成特定事情的目標,像是拿到多益金色證書或工作薪資增加等。這些目標很棒,你應該設一個你想達成的時間。然而在有些情況下,你不該設定成就目標,而是要設定行動目標,行動目標是你設定要花多少時間去做特定事情的目標。以閱讀英文小說為例,雖然這是提升英文最好的方法之一,但是你設定目標每天要讀幾個章節或設定幾個月讀完一本小說,這種設定是錯誤的。只會帶給你壓力,而且可能很容易就放棄了。不如設定一個行動目標:決定每天固定花幾分鐘的時間閱讀小說,也不用管你看了幾頁。對你的目標也要保持彈性。有時候你可能需要減少時間,而有時候你可能會想增加。這樣做,幾個月後,你會很驚訝自己已經讀完了許多。

attainment 成就　admit 錄取　obtain 拿到、獲得
a certain number of 幾個　remain 保持

Love 愛

Love Isn't Just Chemistry.

True love is often mistaken as an emotion, like the butterflies in your stomach, or that chemistry when you first meet someone. While all these feelings are beautiful and thrilling, they are just the tip of the iceberg. True love goes beyond short-lived emotions; it's about the commitment to stick together, even when the going gets tough. It's about choosing each other every day, even when the butterflies have quieted down. It's the promise to stand by each other, to grow together, to work through the difficulties, and to share life's joys and challenges. Love matures over time, and the real essence of love is in the willingness to walk the journey together, no matter what. So, when you say you love someone, it's a promise of your loyalty, patience, understanding, and undying support.

愛不只是化學反應

真愛常常被誤解為一種情感,像是有蝴蝶在胃裡一樣,讓你感到七上八下,又或是你第一次見到某人時的那種化學反應。儘管這些感覺既美好又令人興奮,但其實這些都只是冰山一角。真愛是超越短暫的情感,是即使遭遇困難也能緊緊相依的承諾。是每天都認定彼此,即便那些蝴蝶已經安靜了下來。它是一個相互扶持、一起成長、共同克服困難,與分享人生喜悅和挑戰的承諾。愛會隨著時間而加深,而愛的真正精髓是無論如何都願意和對方一起走下去的意願。所以,當你說你愛一個人時,就是承諾 —— 你的忠誠、耐心、理解和永不動搖的扶持。

emotion 情感　thrilling 令人興奮的　mature 加深
essence 精髓　undying 永不動搖的

Day 16

Grit 恆毅力

Don't Step out of Your Comfort Zone—Stretch Your Comfort Zone.

You know how we sometimes shy away from things that don't come naturally to us? Let's turn that around. Picture your comfort zone as having an elastic band wrapped around it. You want to keep pushing on that band, stretching it outward so that your comfort zone eventually becomes larger. Specifically, how about setting aside a bit of time each week, maybe an hour or so, just to work on something that's a bit of a stretch for you? It could be anything that you feel you're not ace at right now. This isn't about becoming perfect at it overnight but about getting comfortable with being uncomfortable and gradually expanding your comfort zone, you know? Each session, you're stretching your comfort zone, increasing the number of things you can do comfortably. And before you know it, what was once a tough nut to crack starts to feel like second nature. That's how you grow—bit by bit, week by week!

你不用跳脫舒適圈，而是 —— 擴大舒適圈

你知道我們有時會避開自己比較不擅長的事情嗎？讓我們來改變這種情況。想像一下你的舒適圈是用一條彈力帶包圍著。你要持續推動這條帶子，讓它向外伸展，這樣你的舒適圈最終會變得更大。具體來說，每週空出一點時間，可能一個小時左右，做一些超出你能力的事。這可以是任何你覺得自己現在不是很擅長的事。不是要你一夜之間變得完美，只是要你去做一點不舒適的事，並且慢慢地擴張你的舒適圈，懂嗎？每一次的訓練，你都在拓展你的舒適圈，增加你可以舒適做事情的量。而且，在你不知不覺中，那些曾經是棘手的問題開始變成你擅長處理的事情。這就是你成長的方式 —— 一點一點，一週一週！

shy away from 避開、閃躲　set aside 空出、保留
session 次、回　a tough nut to crack 棘手的問題

Day 17

Happiness 快樂

Make Hours Feel Like Minutes.

Let's get into something big—discovering what really excites you. It's crucial to do things that spark your interest and make hours feel like minutes. When you dive into something you love, it adds a special kind of joy to your life. It's possible that you still haven't discovered what you truly love doing, though. So, why not try out new hobbies and activities? Keep an eye out for what gets you really enthusiastic. It might be art, music, writing, reading English novels, or something totally unique to you. The main thing is to find what grabs you, something that you can get totally wrapped up in. Finding your passion isn't just nice, it can seriously boost your mood and overall happiness. So, what are you waiting for? Get out there and see what you can find!

讓好幾個小時變得像只有幾分鐘

我們來討論一些比較大的事 —— 尋找真正能讓你感到興奮的事物。去做一些能誘發你的興趣、讓好幾個小時變得像幾分鐘一樣的事情，是至關重要的。當你投入在自己喜愛的事情中，它會為你的生活增添特別的樂趣。然而，你可能還沒有找到自己真正喜歡做的事。那麼，何不試試看新的興趣和活動呢？好好留意那些能讓你真正充滿熱情的事。可能是藝術、音樂、寫作、閱讀英文小說，或其它冷門的事物而你情有獨鍾。重點是去找那些能吸引你、能讓你全心全意投入的東西。追尋你的熱情不僅是美好而已，還能大大提升你的心情和整體的幸福感。那麼，你還在等什麼？出去看看你能發現什麼吧！

crucial 至關重要的　enthusiastic 熱情的
grab 吸引　passion 熱情

Day 18

Growth 成長

Don't Exhaust Yourself Chasing After Perfection.

You know, perfection is like a mirage. It seems real from a distance, but the closer you get, the more it moves away. It's like climbing a mountain and thinking you've reached the peak, only to find there's yet another peak hiding behind it. The beauty lies in the climb itself, the process of discovering new views, overcoming challenges, and becoming stronger with each step. That's what improvement is all about. It's not about reaching a point of perfection, but about growing, evolving, and getting better each day. So, don't exhaust yourself chasing after perfection; instead aim for improvement. Try to constantly improve by a tiny little bit every day. Get in the habit of asking yourself, "How could I do it a little better this time?" Keep climbing, keep discovering, and keep pushing your limits. That's where real satisfaction and progress are.

不要為了追求完美，而疲憊不堪

你知道嗎？完美就像海市蜃樓。從遠處看似乎很真實，但越靠近，它就離你越遠。就像爬一座山，你以為自己已經到達了頂峰，但卻發現後面還隱藏著另一個山峰。其實美好是在爬山的過程，發現新視野、克服挑戰，以及每走一步都變得更強韌。這就是進步的真諦。不是為了達到完美，而是為了每天都有成長、進展和變得更好。所以，不要為了追求完美而疲憊不堪，而是應該以進步為目標。試著每天都進步一點點，習慣問自己：「這次我要怎麼做才會更好一點？」不斷攀登、不斷探索和不斷挑戰自己的極限。這才是真正的滿足和進步所在。

mirage 海市蜃樓　lie in 是在、在於
process 過程

Day 19

Self-Care 自我關懷

Let Go of Regrets.

Getting rid of regret is like clearing old clutter from your room. It frees up space for new, positive experiences. Holding onto regrets is like carrying a backpack full of stones; it only weighs you down. A good way to overcome regret is to turn it into a learning experience and resolve to change what you're doing, starting now. A common regret people have is that they focus too much on work but not enough on family. Ask yourself, "Have I fallen into this trap?" If you have, then pull out your calendar immediately and schedule regular family time so that you can avoid suffering this regret in the future. You know that family is critically important, so be sure to make it a part of your regular schedule. Whatever you do, though, don't dwell on the regret. Instead, work to ensure that you never experience this exact same regret again. Transforming regret into a lesson and action helps you grow and move forward. Regret no longer!

不再後悔

擺脫後悔就像清理房間的舊雜物一樣,為新的、正面的經驗騰出空間。抱著後悔不放,就像一直背著裝滿石頭的背包,只會讓你感到沉重不堪。克服後悔的好方法是將後悔轉為一種學習經歷,並下定決心從現在開始改變你正在做的事情。人們常後悔的是他們過於專注在工作,而忽略了家庭。問問自己:「我是不是也掉入了這個陷阱?」如果是,那麼立刻拿出你的行事曆,安排固定的家庭時間,這樣你就可以避免未來有這樣的遺憾。你知道家庭是至關重要的,所以一定要把它納入你的常規日程中。不過,無論如何,都不要沉浸在後悔裡。而是要努力確保自己不會再次經歷同樣的遺憾。將後悔轉化為教訓和行動,可以幫助你成長和前進。不再後悔!

get rid of 擺脫　clutter 雜亂的東西　overcome 克服
dwell on 老是想著　transform 轉化

Day 20

Philosophy 人生觀

This Is the One Life You've Got.

Life isn't meant to be lived huddled in a corner, no matter how safe it feels. Life is a great adventure waiting to happen, filled with unexpected and exciting events. The safety of the corner may protect you, but it also limits you. It's outside in the unpredictability, where the miracles happen. It's where you find out what you're truly capable of, where you meet people who change your perspective, where you stumble and fall, but learn how to get back up stronger. Every day offers a new scene in your adventure, a chance to explore something unfamiliar, to learn, to grow, to laugh, and to love. So, step out from that corner, face the unknown with a spark in your eyes, and live a life overflowing with adventure. It's the one life you've got, make it count!

這是你唯一的人生

無論有多麼的安全，人生並不是要一直窩在角落裡過日子。人生是一場即將展開的非凡冒險，充滿了意想不到和令人興奮的事。角落的安全也許能保護你，但也限制了你。不可預測的外面，是奇蹟發生的所在。在那裡，你會發現自己真正的能力、遇到改變你觀點的人、你會絆倒，但也學會如何堅強地重新站起來。每一天都會為你的冒險提供一個新的場景，一個探索未知的機會，去學習、去成長、去笑、去愛。所以，走出那個角落，用你炯炯有神的眼睛去面對未知，過著充滿冒險的生活。這是你唯一的人生，把握它吧！

huddle 窩、縮成一團　stumble 絆倒、跌倒
spark 炯炯有神　overflow with 充滿的

Phase
3
. . . .

Launch Action Steps
展開行動

-from Day 26-

**"It's not what happens to you in life that counts.
Rather, it's what you do about it that really matters."**

「重點不在於你的人生裡發生了什麼事，
而是在面對它時你會怎麼做。」

Gratitude 感恩

Pen Gratitude to Exude Positivity.

How about we bring back a bit of old-school charm with thank-you notes? Once a week, let's take a moment to pen down a few lines to someone who's made a difference in our week. It could be a friend, a teacher, or hey, even the barista who nails your coffee every time. It doesn't have to be fancy, just a simple note or email to say, "Hey, I noticed what you did, and I'm really thankful for it." It's a small act, but it can mean a lot. And you know what? It not only makes their day a bit brighter, but it feels pretty good for us too. It's like a little burst of positivity, and who knows, it might just cause others to show their gratitude, too. Try it!

寫下感謝，散發正念

我們用感謝信，帶回一點老派魅力如何？每週一次，抽點時間寫下幾行字，給那些讓我們這一週過得更好的人。可能是朋友、老師，或是那位每次都能完美做好你咖啡的咖啡師。不需要多花俏，只要一張簡單的便條紙或是電子郵件，說一聲：「嘿，我注意到你所做的一切，我真的很感激。」這樣的小舉動，卻意義重大。你知道嗎？這不但能讓他們的一天更加開心，對我們自己來說也會感覺很好。就像是迸發出一些正能量，而且說不定，這可能也會讓其他人也展現他們的感激。試試看！

old-school charm 老派魅力　barista 咖啡師　nail 完美做好、成功完成
fancy 花俏的、華麗的　burst 迸發、突然增加

Day 22

Conquering Adversity 克服逆境

Even the Best Athletes Have Coaches.

You know that myth that says you should tackle everything alone? Well, that's just not true. Even the best athletes have coaches, right? They get that outside perspective to level up. Needing help isn't a sign you're lacking—it just means you're smart enough to get the right tools. So, if something's bothering you, whether it's your thoughts, skills, or finances, why not seek out an expert? Find a therapist, a coach, or a financial pro. These folks are equipped to help you overcome obstacles and thrive. Bringing in an outside perspective? Sometimes that's the key. It's not about giving up; it's about teaming up to conquer whatever comes your way.

最優秀的運動員也有教練

你聽過「你應該獨自解決一切」的迷思嗎？嗯，這是不對的想法。就算是最優秀的運動員也有教練，對吧？他們透過外部視角來提升自己。需要幫助並不代表你能力不足 —— 而是代表你夠聰明，懂得物色正確的工具。因此，如果有什麼事情困擾著你，無論是你的思緒、技能或財務狀況，何不尋求專家的幫助呢？找治療師、教練或財務專家，他們有能力幫助你克服困難並發展得更好。引進外部視角呢？有時這就是解決問題的關鍵。這不是放棄，而是組隊克服你所面臨的困難。

lacking （能力）不足的　finance 財務
therapist 治療師　thrive 發展得很好、很成功

Learning 學習

The Chance to Truly Master Vocab.

Let me share a little tip about learning English words. A lot of people learn just one meaning of a word and don't realize that most words have multiple meanings. This is why you've probably said, "I know the words, but I don't get the sentence." You probably don't truly understand one or more of those words. So, when reading, if a sentence feels a bit weird even though you feel certain you know all the words, it's a cue to check the dictionary. Maybe there's a common usage of a word you're not aware of. Don't miss this chance to really learn! It's tempting to think you've got the meaning just from context, but that can be tricky, even for native speakers. Always double-check words, even familiar ones, to be sure you're on the right track. It's a small step, but it makes a big difference!

真正學好單字的機會

讓我分享一個關於學習英文單字的小技巧。很多人只會學單字的一個意思,卻沒有意識到大多數的單字本身有很多個意思。這就是為什麼你可能會說:「我看得懂這些單字,但就是搞不懂整句話在講什麼。」其實你應該不是真的知道其中的哪一個或哪幾個單字的意思是什麼。所以,在閱讀時,如果確信自己知道所有的單字,但整個句子讀起來就是感覺怪怪的,這就是在提示你該查字典了。可能是有個單字,它有你所不知道的常見用法。千萬別錯過這個可以真正學好單字的機會!大家很容易認為從上下文就可以推出單字的意思,但其實就算是母語人士,也沒那麼容易。所以,總是要再次查單字,即使是那些你已熟悉的單字,這樣可以確保你走在正確的路上(有正確的理解)。雖然這是一個小步驟,卻會帶來很大的改善。

weird 奇怪的　cue 提示
context 上下文　tricky 很難處理的

Goals & Dreams 目標與夢想

20 Dreams Daily.

Let's talk about a little habit that could be a game changer. Every morning, sometime after you wake up, perhaps as you nibble on your breakfast, write down a list of 20 things you want to achieve. 20 things might sound like a lot, but don't sweat it. Just write down the first 20 things that pop into your head, big or small, such as invest in an index fund, take a trip to Bali Island, develop an app, master the art of coffee making, or start an online business. Avoid looking at what you've written on past days. The idea of the exercise is to see what your subconscious mind thinks is important right now. This exercise will help direct your mind to the goals you truly want and give you the focus and energy to achieve the most important items on the list. Do this exercise every day for 30 days, and your life will never be the same.

每天 20 個夢想

來講一個可能會改變遊戲規則的小習慣。每天早上起床後,可能是你在啃早餐的時候,寫下你想要達成的 20 件事清單。20 件事可能聽起來很多,但不要擔心。只要寫下你第一時間腦海裡浮現的 20 件事,無論大小,例如投資指數基金、去峇里島旅遊、開發一個應用程式、精通咖啡製作藝術,或是開創一個網路事業。不要回頭看你前幾天寫過的內容。這個練習的目的,是為了發現你的潛意識裡現在什麼是重要的。這個練習也會幫助你將注意力集中在真正想要的目標上,讓你集中精神和精力實現清單上最重要的項目。每天做這個練習並持續 30 天,你的人生將會完全不同。

nibble 啃、小口地吃　pop into 在……裡浮現
invest 投資　index fund 指數基金

Love 愛

Don't Set Unrealistic Standards.

It's a simple yet profound truth that no one is perfect. We all come with our strengths and areas we could improve. It's essential to remember this, especially when it comes to relationships. Expecting someone to be perfect sets an unrealistic standard, both for them and for yourself. It can lead to disappointment and unnecessary tension. Instead, it's healthier to embrace and accept each other's imperfections. It's in these imperfect moments, the missteps, and the laughter that follows, where the real bonding happens. It's what makes a relationship genuine and enduring. So, let's be kinder to each other, practice patience, and remember that in a world where no one is perfect, understanding and acceptance are what truly build a solid foundation.

不要設立不切實際的標準

這是一個簡單又奧妙的真理：沒有人是完美的。我們都有自己的優點和需要改進的地方，這一定要記得，尤其是在感情上。期待有個完美的人，只是為對方和自己設立了一個不切實際的標準，這樣可能會帶來失望和不必要的緊繃。而是要去擁抱和接受彼此的不完美，才是健康的心態。也正是這些不完美的時刻、出錯和伴隨而來的笑聲，讓彼此又更親近了。這就是讓感情變得真誠又長久的原因。所以，要對彼此更加友善，練習你的耐心，並記住，在一個沒有人是完美的世界裡，理解和接受才是真正建立堅定根基的因素。

profound 奧妙的、深奧的　tension 緊繃　misstep 出錯
bond 親近　enduring 長久的

Grit 恆毅力

It's Not What Happens...

Life is a mixed bag, with lots of ups and downs. Yet, it's not really about the situations you find yourself in, but rather how you react to them. When life gives you a lemon, you have two choices: to let it defeat you or to make lemonade. Each challenge is a chance to learn and grow, to become stronger and wiser. It's your actions in the face of adversity that say who you truly are. So, no matter what comes your way, choose to face it directly, learn from it, and use it as a stepping stone towards becoming a better version of yourself. Remember! It's not what happens to you in life that counts. Rather, it's what you do about it that really matters.

重點不在發生了什麼⋯⋯

人生是一個大雜燴，有很多起起落落。然而，重點不在你處於什麼樣的情況，而在你如何去應對這些情況。當人生給了你一顆檸檬（檸檬代表：你不想要的東西，像是困難、挫折、挑戰、失敗等），你有兩個選擇：讓它打敗你，或是把它做成甜甜的檸檬水（甜甜的檸檬水代表：你想要的東西，像是順利、成功。即：化逆境為順境）。每一次挑戰都是學習成長的機會，讓你變得更強大、更聰明。應對逆境時的表現會顯露出你真正的樣子。因此，無論你遇到什麼困難，要選擇直接面對，從中學習，用它當你的墊腳石，迎向更好的自己。記住！重點不在於你的人生裡發生了什麼事，而是在面對它時你會怎麼做。

defeat 打敗　wiser 更聰明的
directly 直接地　stepping stone 墊腳石

Happiness 快樂

Experience True Happiness.

One of the best ways to feel truly happy is by giving back and helping others. When you lend a hand, not only do you make someone else's day a little brighter, but you also get this warm and fuzzy feeling inside. It's like a happiness boost for both you and the person you've helped. So, look for ways you can volunteer in your community or simply help out a friend or even a stranger. It doesn't have to be anything big or take much time out of your day. Sometimes, even the smallest act of kindness can make a big difference. When you start to see the smiles on people's faces, you'll understand just how powerful giving back can be. Do something for someone else right now and see how you feel.

感受到真正的快樂

感受到真正快樂的最好方法之一就是回饋與幫助他人。當你伸出援手時,不僅讓別人的一天更美好一些,你的內心也會感到暖呼呼的。這對你和你幫助的人來說,就像幸福感的提升。所以,在你的社群裡尋找可以做志工的方式,或幫助朋友或甚至陌生人。你不需要去做什麼大事或是會耗掉你太多時間的事,有時候,即使是小小的善舉也能帶來大大的改變。當你開始看到人們臉上的笑容時,就會明白回饋的力量有多麼強大。現在就為別人做點什麼,看看你有什麼感受。

give back 回饋　warm and fuzzy 暖呼呼的　volunteer 志工、志願者
community 生活圈、社區、社群

Growth 成長

Unsuccessful Effort Is Another Form of Success.

You know what's cool? Every time you put in some effort, it's like adding a tiny, yet powerful, piece to your life's puzzle. Yeah, sometimes things don't go the way you planned, and it feels like you've been surrounded by obstacles. But guess what? It's not a dead end, it's an avenue to achievement. Even if things don't go well, each effort gives you wisdom. You learn a little something, change the placement of your puzzle pieces, and bam! You're one step closer to getting it next time. It's all about gathering these bits of knowledge from every effort, even the ones that seem to go badly. Also, just because you won't be able to finish the puzzle in one go, don't let that deter you from jumping in or changing your approach. Remember that each effort, successful or not, is still meaningful. If it doesn't work, congrats! You have successfully crossed another method off your list of things to try, which means you're one step closer to hanging that puzzle on the wall. Keep going!

不成功，也是一種成功

你知道什麼很酷嗎？每次你付出一些努力，就好像在你的人生拼圖裡加進一塊小小的，但又強大的拼圖。是的，有時候事情不會按照計畫進行，感覺就像你被阻礙團團包圍。但你猜怎麼著？這不是死路一條，而是成長的大道啊。即使事情沒有進展得很順利，但每一次的努力都會帶給你智慧。你會學到一些東西，改變你拼圖的方式，然後砰！下次就離成功更近一步。重點是從每一次的努力中累積這些點滴知識，即使有些努力似乎沒什麼好結果。還有，不要因為你無法一口氣完成拼圖，而不敢去拼或嘗試其他拼法。記住，每一次的努力，無論成功與否都有意義。如果沒成功，恭喜！在你要嘗試的事情清單中，你已成功地劃掉了一個方法。這表示你距離把拼圖掛到牆上的路，又更近了一步。繼續前進！

tiny 小小的　puzzle 拼圖
surround 團團包圍　gather 累積

Self-Care 自我關懷

Stop Blaming Yourself.

You know, blaming yourself and feeling guilty doesn't help at all. It just makes you feel down and zaps your energy. Letting go of self-blame is like breaking free from invisible chains. Remember, making mistakes is just a part of learning and growing, not a reason to be tough on yourself. Whenever you think, "I messed up," try to pause and ask yourself, "What can I learn from this?" Say you didn't do great in a presentation. Instead of sinking into self-blame, think about how to do better next time or get some feedback. Often, things need more practice than we first think, and that's perfectly okay. What you want to do is turn a tough moment into a chance to grow. Everyone has days when things don't go right, but what matters is how you learn and bounce back from them. Keep growing!

停止自責

你知道嗎？責怪自己、感到內疚是一點幫助也沒有，它只會讓你感到沮喪並消耗你的精力。放下自責就像是從無形的枷鎖中解放出來。記得，犯錯只是學習和成長的一部分，而不是對自己嚴苛的理由。每當你想到「我搞砸了」，試著暫停一下，問自己：「我能從這學到什麼？」比如說你在一次簡報中表現不佳，與其陷入自責，不如去想下次要怎麼做才會更好，或請教別人的意見。很多事需要的練習，常常會比我們最初想的還要更多，這很正常。你要做的就是把艱難的時刻變為成長的機會。每個人都會有事情不順利的時候，但重要的是你如何從中學習並重振旗鼓。繼續成長吧！

zap 消耗、破壞　invisible 無形的
mess up 搞砸　sink 陷入

Philosophy 人生觀

The View Is Much Better from the Top.

It's tempting to wish that life were easier, or that things were cheaper, but that's like hoping a mountain changes its height so it's easier to climb. It's a passive approach. However, aspiring to be better and have more is like training yourself to climb higher peaks, or saving up for what you desire. It's taking an active approach that gives you the power to improve your life. Life's going to throw challenges either way, but by planning to be better, you're essentially gearing up to meet those challenges head-on. So, whenever you find yourself wishing for things to be easier or cheaper, catch yourself. Turn that wish towards personal growth and increased earning instead. Trust me, the view is much better from the top, and the sense of accomplishment when you can afford what you want is awesome.

從高點看風景會更美

人們渴望生活變得更輕鬆，或是東西變得更便宜，而這就像希望一座山改變高度，好讓我們能更輕鬆地攀登上去。這是一種被動的態度。然而，你追求變得更好，擁有更多，就像是訓練自己去攀登更高的山峰，或是為了自己想要的東西去存錢一樣。採取主動的態度，會給你改善人生的力量。不管怎樣，人生都會給我們帶來挑戰。但計畫去變得更好，基本上你就做好了迎接這些挑戰的準備。所以，每當你發現自己希望事物變得更加容易或更加便宜時，抓住自己制止這個念頭。將這種希望轉換成個人成長和提高收入。相信我，從更高的點看風景會更美，而能買得起你想要的東西時，那種成就感是無與倫比的。

aspire 追求　peak 山峰
gear up 準備　a sense of accomplishment 成就感

Phase
4
. . . .

Gradually Advance
逐步前進

"With every step taken with grit,

doubt falls further behind, and your dreams come closer."

-from Day 36-

「每一步都堅定地走，

疑慮就會落後更多，而你的夢想也會更近。」

Day 31

Gratitude 感恩

The Currency of Gratitude Is Unlimited.

Gratitude is indeed a special kind of currency, one that doesn't disappear no matter how much you spend. It's a perspective that allows you to see the value in what you have, the people around you, and even the seemingly small moments in life. The beautiful thing is, the more you spend this currency by expressing your thankfulness, the richer you become in happiness and contentment. It's like an investment that only grows over time, never losing its value. And the cool part? There's no limit to how much of this currency you can make. Every moment presents an opportunity to appreciate and feel grateful for the good things in your life. It's a habit that not only improves your own life but also makes the world around you a bit brighter.

感激是用不完的錢幣

感激真的是一種特殊錢幣,無論你花了多少都不會消失。這樣的視角會讓你看到價值,在你擁有什麼、你周遭的人,甚至是生活裡那些看起來不起眼的片刻。美妙的是,你花越多這種錢幣來表達你的感激之情,你就越有富饒的快樂與滿足。它就像一個隨著時間推移只會增值,而永不貶值的投資。那吸引人的部分是什麼?就是你可以無限量的賺取這種錢幣。無時無刻都有機會,讓你為生活美好的事物感到珍惜與感激。這個習慣不只能改善你的生活,還能讓你周遭的世界變得更明亮一些。

currency 錢幣、貨幣　disappear 消失
perspective 視角　brighter 更明亮的

Day 32

Conquering Adversity 克服逆境

Take It Step by Step.

Feeling overwhelmed? I get it. When you're facing something huge, it's like staring at a mountain and thinking, "How am I gonna climb that?" But here's the thing: Don't look at the whole mountain—just focus on the next few steps. Break that big, scary problem into smaller, manageable pieces. Then, start knocking them out, one by one. Each step you take? That's a win! And it adds up. Before you know it, you'll look back and see how far you've come. So, remember, you don't have to solve everything at once. Take it step by step, and you'll get there in the end. Cool, isn't it?

一步一步來吧

覺得壓力山大嗎？我懂。當你面對巨大的問題時，就像在盯著一座山看，在想「我怎麼可能爬得上去？」但其實是這樣的：你不要去看那一整座山，你只要專注在接下來的幾步。把那個又大又可怕的問題拆解成更小、更容易處理的小塊。接著，開始將它們一一擊倒。而你踏出的每一步？那可都是一場勝利！而且都會累積起來。當你注意到時，你再回頭看看自己前進了多少。所以，你要記得，不用一次解決所有的問題。而是一步一步來，最後你就會到達目的地。很棒，對吧？

overwhelmed 負荷大到難以承受的、壓力山大的
stare 盯　scary 可怕的　knock out 擊倒

Learning 學習

Seek Multiple Benefits.

Whatever you're doing, always aim to "kill at least two birds with one stone." Constantly seeking and taking shortcuts often leads to wasted time without gaining anything of value. Take test-taking, for instance. If you genuinely focus on improving your abilities, you won't just pass the test; you'll also function better in your field afterward. It's like when you exercise, you're not just building muscle, you're also improving your overall health. So, always look for ways to maximize the benefits of your efforts. This approach not only saves you time but also ensures that you get the most out of your hard work. Remember, it's not just about working hard; it's about working smart.

追求一舉數得

無論你在做什麼,總要力求「一舉兩得或一舉數得」。不斷地尋找和採取捷徑,往往只是浪費時間,並且一無所獲。以考試來說吧,如果你真正專注在提升自己的能力,那你不只是能通過考試,之後在與這考試有關的專業領域裡,你也能夠發揮更好的能力。這就像運動,你不僅在鍛鍊肌肉,而且也在改善你的整體健康。因此,永遠要找尋方法,來最大化你努力的效益。這種方法不但能節省你的時間,也確保你的勤奮付出可以得到最大的回報。記住,不只是要努力地去做,更是要聰明地去做。

constantly 不斷地　genuinely 真正地
maximize 最大化　ensure 確保

Day 34

Goals & Dreams 目標與夢想

Don't Just Focus on "What's in It for Me?"

Listen, when it comes to goals, it's not just about the end game—the thing you want to have or the place you want to get to. Nah, it's way deeper than that. The true value is who you become while you're reaching for that goal. I mean, sure, scoring that college acceptance or getting that job is awesome. But the person you evolve into? That's the real prize. You learn, you struggle, you adapt, and all that shapes you into someone better. So, don't just focus on the "what will I get" part. Shift that thinking, and ask yourself, "What will I become?" Because, trust me, the growth along the way? That's what you'll carry with you, long after you've achieved that goal.

不要只專注在「我會得到什麼」

聽著，談到目標，不只是終點 —— 你想擁有的東西或你想到達的地方。不，比那更深遠。真正的價值是你在達成目標的過程中會成為什麼樣的人。我的意思是，當然，獲得大學錄取或得到一份工作很棒。然而你成為了怎樣的一個人呢？那才是你真正賺到的東西。你學習、奮鬥、適應，所有的這些都會把你塑造成一個更好的人。因此，不要只專注在「我會得到什麼」這一點。改變你的思維，問問自己「我會成為什麼樣的人？」因為，相信我喔，你這一路上的成長呢？那是在達成目標之後，將會伴隨著你的東西。

way 更　score 獲得
evolve 成為　struggle 奮鬥

Day 35

Love 愛

Before You Get Angry...

It's quite easy to jump to conclusions when your other half says or does something that irks you. However, it's essential to pause and make sure that you've understood their intentions correctly. Misunderstandings are a common part of relationships, and they can lead to unnecessary anger if not clarified. Before you say something you'll regret, take a moment to ask them about their true intentions. More often than not, you'll find that they meant something entirely different from what you initially thought. When they clarify themselves, believe them. It's a simple yet powerful way to maintain harmony and mutual respect in relationships. This habit promotes open communication and prevents minor issues from becoming significant issues.

在你發火前……

當你的另一半說了或做了一些讓你不爽的事情時，你很容易馬上就下定論。但是，其實你有必要先暫停一下，確認你已經正確理解他們的意圖。誤解是感情關係裡很常見的一部分，如果沒有先搞清楚，就很容易導致不必要的生氣。在你說出會讓自己後悔的話之前，花一點時間問問他們真正的意圖是什麼。大部分的時候，你會發現他們真正的用意與一開始認定的想法完全不同。而當他們澄清自己的意圖時，你也要相信他們。這是一個簡單又有用的方法，來維持感情關係裡的和諧與相互尊重。這樣的習慣有助於坦誠溝通，防止小問題變成大問題。

irk 讓 ... 不爽　intention 意圖　clarify 搞清楚
promote 促進、有助於　minor 小的

Day 36

Grit 恆毅力

Leave Doubt Behind You.

Picture life as a long marathon filled with the highs of achievement and the lows of uncertainties. Now, imagine your dreams as the finish line you're working to reach. The pace you run this marathon is not about speed, but endurance, and that enduring pace is fueled by grit. Grit keeps your legs moving when doubt tries to slow you down. With every step taken with grit, doubt falls further behind, and your dreams come closer. It's about outrunning the whisper of doubt with the loud echo of grit, every step of the way. So, put on your shoes, set a pace filled with determination, and run towards your dreams, leaving doubt behind.

將懷疑拋在身後

把生活想像成一場漫長的馬拉松,充滿了成就的高峰和不確定性的低谷。現在,想像你的夢想是你努力想要到達的終點線。進行這場馬拉松的步伐不在於速度,而在於耐力,並且這持續的步伐是靠恆毅力在推動。當自我懷疑要讓你慢下來時,恆毅力會讓你的雙腿繼續前進。每一步都堅定地走,懷疑就會落後更多,而你的夢想也會更近。這是在講一路上的每一步,都用恆毅力的響亮回音來蓋過自我懷疑的低語。所以,穿上你的鞋子,開始並維持堅定的步伐,朝著你的夢想奔跑,將疑慮拋在身後。

pace 步伐　endurance 耐力　fuel by 靠⋯⋯推動
whisper 低語　determination 堅定

Happiness 快樂

Train Your Mind to Focus on the Present.

You've probably heard people talk about the benefits of mindfulness meditation before. It's such a good habit to get into. By practicing mindfulness, you can train your mind to focus on the present moment, which can significantly reduce stress and boost your overall happiness. You don't have to sit there for hours, either. Simply taking a few minutes each day to focus on your breath or practicing some deep breathing exercises can make a huge difference. Even just taking a few moments to pause, breathe, and be present can be an incredibly powerful tool in creating a happier, more peaceful life. Right now, close your eyes and take 5 slow breaths, counting like this: breathe in for 4, hold for 4, breathe out for 4, hold for 4. Repeat 5 times. See? You feel better already, don't you?

訓練心思專注當下

你大概已經聽過有人講正念冥想的好處。這是一個非常值得養成的好習慣。透過練習正念，你可以訓練心思專注在當下，這可以明顯地減少壓力並提高整體的快樂。你不需要坐在那裡幾個小時。只需每天花幾分鐘專注於呼吸或練習吐納，就會產生很大的改善。即使只是花一點時間暫停下來、呼吸並專注在當下，就會是非常強大的工具，來創造更快樂、更祥和的生活。現在，閉上眼睛，慢慢地做 5 次吐納，按照這樣的循環：一是吸氣（心裡從 1 數到 4），二是屏住氣息（心裡從 1 數到 4），三是吐氣（心裡從 1 數到 4），四是屏著氣息數到 4。再回到一，重複 5 次這樣的循環。你看，現在感覺是不是好多了呢？

mindfulness meditation 正念冥想　train 訓練
reduce 減少　boost 提高

Day 38

Growth 成長

Green & Growing or Brown & Dying.

Hey, you know what they say, right? Life's always in motion. You're either getting better, or you're falling behind. Think of yourself as a plant—either green and growing or brown and withering. Trust me, nothing in life stays the same; it's like a river, always flowing. So, make sure you're swimming in the right direction! Whether it's your grades, your friendships, or even your personal goals, always aim to improve. Even the small steps count, you know. Just don't get too comfy and think you've got it all figured out because there's always room to grow. So, let's focus on the here and now, make those wise choices, and keep on climbing. You're capable of so much; don't let yourself forget it.

綠油油成長，還是枯黃凋零？

嘿，你知道大家都怎麼說吧？人生就是一直在變動，你要不變得更好，要不就會被拋在後頭。把自己想像成一棵植物 —— 要嘛綠油油地生長，要嘛就是枯黃凋謝。相信我，人生沒有什麼是永遠不變的，就像一條河，總是在流動。所以，確保你正游向對的方向！不管是你的成績、友誼，甚至是你的個人目標，都要力求進步。即使是小小的進步也很重要，懂嗎？也不要覺得自己已有成就而太過安逸，因為總有成長的空間。因此，讓我們專注於當下，做出明智的選擇，繼續攀登。你的潛力十足，別讓自己忘了這一點。

motion 變動　wither 枯黃凋謝
flow 流動　comfy 安逸的、舒適的

Day 39

Self-Care 自我關懷

Tailor Your Life.

Knowing yourself is about figuring out your unique traits. Honestly observing your actions (or asking someone who's close to tell you) is the key to doing so. Take sleep, as an example. Some people are full of energy with just a few hours of sleep, while others need a solid 8 or 9 hours to feel their best. When it comes to learning, everyone's different too. You might be a visual learner who needs to see things, an auditory learner who needs to hear things, or maybe you're tactile and learn only by doing. And hey, some people are go-getters, always self-motivated, while others don't get off the sofa unless they get a push from others. If you do need a push, be sure to find someone who will push you. By understanding who you are, you can tailor your life, learning, and work to suit you best. It also means not being too hard on yourself. So, discovering your true self is the secret weapon that can help you improve your quality of life, learning effectiveness, or work efficiency!

為自己量身訂做

認識自己是要發現自己獨特的地方。誠實地觀察你的行為（或是詢問與你親近的人），是發現自己的關鍵。以睡眠為例，有些人只需要幾小時就精力充沛，而有些人需要整整 8、9 個小時才感覺比較好。至於學習，每個人也不一樣。你可能是需要看到東西的視覺型學習者、需要聽到東西的聽覺型學習者，或者你是觸覺型的，要透過實際動手做來學習。嘿，還有，有些人就是積極進取，總會自我激勵，也有些人是需要別人推，才會離開沙發。如果你需要人推，就要找到能推動你的人。透過了解你是誰，你可以為生活、學習和工作來量身訂做最適合你的作法。這也表示你不要對自己太苛刻。所以，找出自己是怎樣的人——是讓你增加生活品質、提高學習成效或工作效率的祕密武器！

tailor 量身訂做　visual 視覺型的
auditory 聽覺型的　tactile 觸覺型的

Day 40

Philosophy 人生觀

Take the Road Less Traveled.

"Success is doing the opposite of what everybody else is doing." It's quite an interesting notion, isn't it? The idea that taking a different path could lead to success. It's like taking a less crowded street and discovering a shortcut. The world is full of "accepted wisdoms" that often go unchallenged, mostly because they've been around for ages. But here's where it gets exciting—when you pause and question the usual way of doing things, you're already on a path less traveled. You start to see things from a fresh angle, which is often the starting point of innovation. It's not about opposing the common just to be contrary, but about evaluating things with your own lens, gathering your own evidence. So, whenever you hear a "that's how it's always been done," question it instead of blindly following it.

走上一條沒什麼人走的路

「成功就是做大家會做的事的相反。」 這是個很有趣的觀點，對吧？這在講即便走不同的路也可能會走向成功的概念。就像在走一條沒那麼多人走的街道，然後發現了一條小路。這個世界充滿了「公認的智慧」，這些智慧通常不會受到質疑，主因是它們已存在了許久。但這正是讓人興奮的地方 —— 當你暫停下來，質疑最普遍的做事方式，你已經走上了一條沒什麼人在走的道路。你開始用全新的角度看待事物，而這往往是創新的起點。這並不是為了反對常態而反對，而是要你用自己的視角來評價事物，匯集你自己的憑據。所以，每當你聽到「這就是我們一直以來的作法」時，請質疑它，而不是盲目地跟隨。

notion 觀點　crowded 多人走的、擁擠的　contrary 反對的
evaluate 評價　gather 匯集

Phase
5

· · · · · · · · · · · ·

Persistently Execute

堅持執行

"When the going gets tough, and you're ready
to throw in the towel, that's exactly when you
should challenge yourself to do just one more."

-from Day 46-

「當局面變得困難，你準備認輸時，
這正是你要挑戰自己再做一次的時候。」

Day 41

Gratitude 感恩

Share Gratitude at the Dining Table.

How about making mealtime more than just about food? While everyone's munching, let's get into the habit of sharing one thing we're each grateful for. It doesn't have to be big—maybe you aced a quiz, or you just enjoyed a workout at the gym. This isn't just about saying thanks, it's about feeling that warmth spread around the table. It's pretty cool how sharing a simple piece of your day can make the food taste better and the bonds stronger. Plus, hearing what others appreciate can open your eyes to little blessings you might not have noticed. It's like a daily dose of feel-good right in the middle of the hustle and bustle. Let's give it a go and see how our meals and our days get a whole lot richer.

餐桌上的感激分享

讓用餐時間不局限於食物如何？當大家都在咀嚼食物的時候，我們來養成分享一件自己感激事物的習慣。沒有一定要是大事 —— 可能是你的小考很高分，或者你剛享受了健身房的訓練。這不只是說聲謝謝而已，也是在感受溫暖瀰漫在餐桌上。很棒的是分享一天中的簡單片段能讓食物變得更加美味，也讓彼此的關係更牢固。再加上聽聽別人感激什麼，可以讓你睜開雙眼，發現自己之前可能沒有注意到的小確幸。這就像是在匆忙中的一劑日常感覺良好的藥物。試一試，看它如何讓我們的一餐和一天變得更加豐富。

munch 咀嚼、啃　ace 考得很好、考滿分　blessing 幸事
dose 一劑　hustle and bustle 匆匆忙忙

Conquering Adversity 克服逆境

Write Down Your Thoughts to Untangle Your Mind.

Ever feel like your thoughts are just swimming around in your head? We all get that way sometimes. One really good way to sort things out is to grab a notebook and start jotting down whatever's on your mind—your feelings, your worries, whatever it is. It's like you're decluttering a super messy room. Once you've got all those thoughts out of your head and down on paper, they're not all jumbled up in your mind anymore. You can actually see them right in front of you. You might even start to see patterns or figure out what your next steps should be. So, why not give it a try? Just let the words flow. It's a really useful way to help you navigate through the tough times.

寫下思緒，理出頭緒

有沒有感覺過你的想法只是在你的腦海裡游來游去？我們都有這樣的時候。一個理出頭緒很好的方法就是拿一本筆記簿，開始摘要記下你腦裡的任何想法——你的感受、你的擔憂或其他任何事情。這就像你正在清理一個非常凌亂的房間一樣。一旦你把這些想法從大腦裡抽出來，並且記在紙上，在你的腦海裡它們便不再這麼混亂。你可以真正地看到它們就在你的面前，甚至你可能開始看到了一些共同點，或者想通下一步該做什麼。所以，何不試試呢？不要想太多，就寫下來。這是一個非常有用的方法，能夠幫助你在艱難時刻確定方向。

sort out 整理、歸整　declutter 清理
jumbled 混亂的、亂七八糟的　navigate 導航、確定方向

111

Learning 學習

Don't Wait Until "Ready"!

No matter how good your English vocabulary, grammar, pronunciation, or writing is, you might feel like it's not good enough to use. Of course, you can always learn new words and deepen your understanding of the words you already know. But remember, don't let the fear of not being "good enough" or not being "ready" hold you back. If you do, you might find yourself stuck in a loop of inaction. The truth is you learn by doing. Every mistake is a lesson that brings you one step closer to fluency. So, go ahead, use what you know, and don't be afraid to make mistakes. Embrace the learning process and watch as your English skills blossom. You've got this!

不要等到「準備好了」才開始

無論你的英文字彙、文法、發音或寫作有多好，你可能會覺得還不夠好到可以使用它。當然，你可以隨時學習新單字，並加深對已知單字的理解。但要記住，不要讓「不夠好」或「還沒準備好」的恐懼來阻礙你。如果你被恐懼阻礙，你可能會發現自己卡在一個無所作為的循環裡。事實是，你要透過使用英文來學習。每一個錯誤都是經驗，讓你距離流利、熟練更近一步。所以，放膽使用你已經知道的英文，不要害怕用錯。擁抱學習的過程，見證你的英語能力開花結果。你一定做得到！

stuck 卡住的、陷入的　loop 循環
inaction 沒有作為、沒有行動　blossom 開花結果

Goals & Dreams 目標與夢想

Remain Open and Welcome Change.

Listen, when you're starting any new adventure, it's super important to know what you want, alright? Think of it like this: you're going on a road trip—you know the end point, but you can get there in many different ways, each leading to a different adventure. So, don't be inflexible and stick to the first path you planned on taking. Our world's packed with so many options that can be just as awesome as your end goal. Keep your mind open, be willing to accept changes, and soak up the experience. You'll see, sometimes these unplanned routes end up being the best part of the whole journey. You still reach your destination, but the whole ride was way more interesting and rewarding, wasn't it?

保持開放，接受變化

聽著,當你開始任何新的冒險時,知道自己想要什麼是超級重要的,對吧? 可以這樣想:你要去公路旅行 —— 你知道終點在哪,然而你有很多條路線可以到那裡,每一條都會帶來不同的冒險。所以,你不要死板,固執只走一開始就計畫好的路線。我們的世界充滿了許多的選擇,而這些選擇可能跟你的最終目標一樣棒。要保持開放的心態,願意接受變化,並且吸收經驗。你會發現,有時候這些計畫外的路線最終成為整個旅程中最棒的部分。你仍然到達了終點,但這整個旅程是不是更有趣、更有收穫了呢?

114

adventure 冒險　inflexible 死板的　packed 充滿的
option 選擇　soak up 吸收

Love 愛

Jealousy and Control Are Like Relationship Poison.

If you're aiming for a rock-solid relationship, you've gotta build it on trust. That doesn't just mean not cheating, by the way. It's about being each other's rock: the person who's there no matter what life throws at you. Be consistent, don't make promises you can't keep, and whatever you do, be honest—even when it's hard. But trust isn't just about being trusted; it's also about trusting them. Let them have their own space and friendships, and don't stress out over the small stuff. Jealousy and control are like relationship poison. And hey, mistakes happen, so forgiveness is key. When you've got that trust, you've got a love that can withstand just about anything. Keep that in mind!

嫉妒和控制是感情的毒藥

如果你的目標是建立一段堅如磐石的感情關係，那你必須將它建立在信任的基礎上。對了，這不僅僅是指不出軌，而是要成為彼此的磐石：無論人生遇到什麼難題或阻礙，彼此都是那個永遠在那裡的人。要始終如一，不要給無法兌現的承諾。無論做什麼，都要誠實 —— 就算再怎麼困難也要做到。然而，信任不只是在講你被他們信任，你也要去信任他們。讓他們有自己的空間和友誼，不要為了小事而壓力太大。嫉妒和控制就像感情的毒藥。對了，人難免會犯錯，所以原諒也是關鍵。當有了這種信任，你們就擁有了幾乎能承受任何考驗的愛。記住這一點！

poison 毒藥　rock-solid 堅如磐石的
cheat 出軌　withstand 承受

Grit 恆毅力

Just One More.

When the going gets tough, and you're ready to throw in the towel, that's exactly when you should challenge yourself to do just one more. It could be anything—one more lap around the track, one more math problem, or one more run-through of your presentation. It's about pushing past that initial "I can't" and finding out that you actually can. This isn't about overdoing it but about proving to yourself that you've got more in you than you thought. You'll be surprised how often that "one more" becomes the step that makes all the difference. It's like a little nudge to your confidence each time, showing you that, yes, you've got this! And that's a feeling that's worth every bit of effort. Keep it up!

只要再一次

當局面變得困難，你準備認輸時，這正是你要挑戰自己再做一次的時候。任何事都可以這樣做——再跑一圈賽道、再解一道數學題目，或再排練一次你的簡報。這是在講超越最初的「我做不到」，而發現自己實際上可以做到。這不是說要做得太過頭，而是在講向自己證明，你比自己想像的更有能力。你會驚訝地發現，那個「再來一次」常常就是改變一切的決定性一步。它就像是一個小推力，每次都對你展現信心，是的，你能做到！而這種感覺讓一切努力都值得。繼續加油！

lap （跑道的）一圈　run-through 排練、排演
overdo 做得過頭、過火　nudge 推力、輕推

Happiness 快樂

Transform Your Mood.

You know what's a game changer for your mood and energy? Getting regular exercise. Now, I'm not saying you have to run a marathon or anything. Just find something that gets you moving and makes you happy. It could be doing air squats, hiking, or even just a walk around the block. The key is to make it a regular part of your routine, and not just something you do once in a blue moon. It's amazing how much better you'll feel, both physically and mentally, when you stay active. And hey, it's a great way to clear your head and de-stress too. So, go on, find that activity that makes you feel alive, and make it a must for your day. You got this!

翻轉你的心情

你知道什麼可以完全翻轉你的心情和精力嗎？那就是規律運動。嗯，我不是說你要去跑個馬拉松或其他難度那麼高的。只要找一些能讓你動起來，而且你會開心的活動就好。可以是深蹲、健行，或甚至只是在街區周圍散步。重點是要讓它成為你日常生活的一部分，而不是久久才做一次。很棒的是當你有在持續活動時，你的身體和心理都會感覺更好。嘿，這也是你清空腦袋和減輕壓力的絕佳方法。所以，去做吧，找到那個可以讓你充滿活力的活動，並且讓它成為你一天中不可或缺的部分。你可以的！

regular 規律的　air squat 深蹲
once in a blue moon 久久才一次地　de-stress 減輕壓力

Growth 成長

Add Fuel to Your Growth Fire.

Imagine your personal growth as a campfire. The more wood you add, the bigger and warmer it gets. Similarly, the pace at which you grow significantly depends on how often and how much effort you put into your personal growth fire. It's really straightforward—the more time and energy you dedicate, the quicker and fuller your growth. It's about showing up every day, even if some days are harder than others. Let's say you want to get a six-pack. If you do crunches every day, and gradually increase the number of reps you do each time, you'll have washboard abs in no time! Each effort, no matter how small, adds fuel to your fire. It's a continuous effort, sometimes exhausting, but it's so rewarding. So, keep piling on the efforts, keep fueling your fire, and you'll see how wonderfully warm and bright it can get.

為你的成長火焰添加燃料

把你的個人成長想像成營火，你加越多的木頭，火就越大越暖。同樣地，你成長的速度在很大程度上是取決於你投入多久和努力多少在個人成長的火焰中。這是很直接的 —— 你付出的時間和精力越多，你的成長就會越快越徹底。重點是每天都要這樣做，即使有的時候會比其他時候更辛苦一些。好比說你想要擁有六塊肌。如果你每天都做捲腹運動，並逐漸增加每一次的次數，你很快就會擁有洗衣板般的腹肌！每一次的努力，無論多小，都會為你的成長火焰增加燃料。這是持續性的努力，有時會讓人筋疲力盡，但也會很有收穫。所以，繼續下工夫，繼續催動你的火，你會看到它會變得有多麼溫暖和明亮。

dedicate 付出、專攻　crunch 捲腹運動　rep 次（數）、下
washboard abs 洗衣板般的腹肌　rewarding 有收穫的

Self-Care 自我關懷

Don't Kid Yourself.

Remember, it's really easy to fool yourself. That's why it's so important to always be true to who you are. Think of honesty with yourself as a map guiding you on your journey. It keeps you on track, even when shortcuts seem tempting. A good habit is to regularly reflect on your feelings and decisions. Like, when you're deciding on a major or a profession, ask yourself: "Do I want to do this because I genuinely like it or simply to satisfy my family's wishes?" This self-check helps you make choices that truly match your interests and values. Every time you're honest with yourself, you're paving the way to a life that's genuinely fulfilling and authentic to who you are. Always remember to stay true to yourself—it's the best path to take!

不要騙自己

記得，欺騙自己其實很容易，這是為什麼始終對你自己真誠如此重要。把對自己的誠實視為在旅途中指引你的地圖。它能讓你保持在正軌上，即使捷徑看起來很誘人。一個好習慣是去定期反思你的感想和決定。例如，當你決定選擇專業主修或工作職業時，問問自己：「我這樣做是因為我真的喜歡它，還是只是為了滿足家人的願望？」這樣的自我檢查可以幫助你做出真正符合你興趣和價值觀的選擇。每當你對自己誠實時，就是為真正的滿足、真實的你的人生在鋪路。永遠記得要忠於自己──這是走最好的路！

reflect 反思　match 符合
authentic 真正的

Philosophy 人生觀

Label Wisely.

To paraphrase Shakespeare, "Nothing is good or bad, but the way you think about it makes it good or bad." We have the power to give meaning to things around us. Everything's like a blank canvas, and we get to decide what color, shape, or image it holds. If you label something as bad or good, that's the reality you create for yourself. It's all in the labels, the meanings you attach. For instance, if you label a setback as a "failure," it might bring you down. But call it a "lesson," and it will teach you something. You learn, you grow, and you're happier for it. The labels you choose create your emotions and experiences. So, whenever you're about to label something, take a pause, and choose a label that brings positivity and growth. Your happiness truly is in your hands, or should I say, in your labels.

聰明地貼上標籤

用莎士比亞的話來說，「事物本身無好壞，只是你對它的看法決定了它是好是壞。」我們有能力去賦予周遭事物的意義。每件事都像一張空白的畫布，我們決定它的顏色、形狀或圖案。如果你給一件事貼上不好的、或好的標籤，那就是你給自己創建的事實。這一切都在於標籤上，你所附加的意義。舉個例子，如果你把一次的挫折貼上「失敗」的標籤，這可能會讓你感到沮喪。但如果你稱它是「教訓」，那它就會教你一些東西，讓你有所學習、成長，也讓你更加快樂。你所選擇的標籤會創建你的情緒和體驗。因此，每當你要給一件事情貼上標籤時，停下來，選一個能帶來正向和成長的標籤。你的快樂確實掌握在你的手上，或者應該說，在你的標籤上。

paraphrase 換句話說　canvas 畫布、帆布
attach 附加　setback 挫折

Phase
6

. . . .

Integrate into Life
融入生活

**"Whenever you glance at it,
you'll have a visual nudge of the good stuff in your life."**

-from Day 51-

「每次一看到它，你就會得到一個視覺上的提醒，
讓你想到生活中的美好事物。」

Day 51

Gratitude 感恩

Gratitude Collage Keeps You Positive.

How about making a gratitude collage? Grab some photos and bits and pieces that remind you of what you're thankful for. It's like a mood board but for gratitude. Assemble them into a cool collage and hang it up where you'll see it all the time. Whenever you glance at it, you'll have a visual nudge of the good stuff in your life. It could be snaps from a trip, a ticket stub from a concert, even a doodle from your little cousin. Seeing your personal collection of happy moments can brighten your day and keep those thankful vibes strong. It's a simple way to keep your spirits up and remember the cool things that make life sparkle.

感恩拼貼讓你保持好心情

要不要嘗試製作感恩拼貼畫呢?拿一些會提醒你感激的事物的照片和其他小物件。這有點像是心情貼板,但是是用來提醒感恩的。把它們組合成一幅很棒的拼貼畫,並且掛在你隨時都可以看得到的地方。每次一看到它,你就會得到一個視覺上的提醒,讓你想到生活中的美好事物。它可以是旅行時的快照、演唱會的票根,甚至是你小表弟的塗鴉。看著你個人快樂時刻的收集,可以讓你的一天變得更好,並讓你時刻保持感恩的心情。這是一個簡單的方式,讓你保持正向好心情,並記得那些讓人生閃亮發光的美好事情。

assemble 組合成　glance 看到（極短的時間）　snap 快照
doodle 塗鴉　sparkle 閃亮發光

Conquering Adversity 克服逆境

Gotta Have a Plan B.

Look, not everything's gonna go the way you want it to, right? So, when you hit a wall, don't just stand there staring at it—take another route. That's where your Plan B comes in. Yeah, it's more than just a cool phrase; it's a lifesaver when things go badly. Being flexible isn't a sign of weakness, it's actually being smart and ready for whatever life throws at you. So, if Plan A fails, don't sweat it. Adapt and move on with Plan B. It's kinda like having a spare tire in the car. You hope you never have to use it, but you're really glad it's there when you need it. Keep rolling, you got this.

總是要有 B 計畫

注意，事情不會總是都按照你想的那樣發展，對吧？所以，當你碰壁時，不要只是站在那裡盯著它看，試試別的路吧。這時就是需要你的 B 計畫（備案）了。是的，它不只是一個很酷的術語，當事情進展得不好的時候，它是你的救星。懂得變通不是軟弱的表現，而是聰明的表現，是在為人生隨時會遇到的任何事情做好準備。所以，萬一 A 計畫失敗了，不用擔心。調整並用 B 計畫來做。就像車上有個備胎一樣，你希望永遠不會用到它，但是當你需要的時候，你會很欣慰有它在。繼續前進，你可以的！

hit a wall 碰壁　route 路、路線
lifesaver 救星　spare tire 備胎

Learning 學習

Keep It Fresh.

Learning English should be fun and something you look forward to, not a chore. If you've tried a method for a while but it's just not clicking, don't force it. It might not be the right fit for you at this moment, and that's okay. You might find that it works better for you down the line. The same goes for methods you used to enjoy but now find tiresome. Give yourself permission to switch things up. There are so many different ways to learn, so don't limit yourself. The key is to keep things fresh and exciting. That way, you'll stay motivated and eager to learn more. Remember, the best method is the one that works for you right now!

保持學習的新鮮感

學習英文應該要好玩,是你會期待的事情,而不是一件無聊的差事。如果你試了一種學習方法一陣子,但怎麼試都沒有預期的成效,就不要勉強了。這個方法可能還不適合現在的你,但沒關係。說不定它會對之後的你來說很有用。同理,如果有個學習方式是你以前很喜歡,但現在覺得很膩,那就允許自己換個新方式。學習的方法有很多種,所以不要限制自己。重點是要讓學習這件事保持新鮮感和興奮感,這樣你才會一直很有動力,並且渴望學到更多。記住,最好的方法就是現在最適合你的方法!

chore 無聊的差事、雜務　tiresome 讓人覺得膩的、厭倦的
permission 允許　switch 換過、轉換　eager 渴望的

Goals & Dreams 目標與夢想

Don't Just Help Others Achieve Their Dreams.

If you don't have your own goals, you'll end up working hard to help someone else achieve their dreams. And guess what? Their goals are designed to make the goal setter's life awesome, not yours. You must have your own goals, regardless of the stage of life you're in. For instance, parents often make their goals about their children, which causes them to sacrifice their needs for their kids' needs. As a parent, be sure to have personal goals, too. That way, when your kids leave home, you won't have such an empty feeling inside. Also, when you retire, make sure to keep setting goals so that you don't just mope around the house. For example, you're never too old to learn a new language or learn how to use the latest tech. Research shows that doing these activities increases levels of fulfillment, health, and even longevity. With goals, you'll maintain your sense of personal dignity and experience a sense of accomplishment whenever you achieve something new.

不要只是幫別人實現夢想

如果你沒有自己的目標,最後你只是努力在幫別人實現他們的夢想。你猜怎麼著?他們的目標不是為了你的生活而設,而是為他們自己的生活變得更加美好。無論你處於人生的哪個階段,你都必須要有自己的目標。例如,父母常常將他們的目標投放在孩子身上,這導致他們為了孩子所需而犧牲了自己的需要。身為父母,也一定要有個人目標。這樣,當你的孩子離開家時,你的內心就不會那麼空虛。還有,當你退休時,一定要繼續設定目標,這樣你就不會只是在家裡悶悶不樂。例如,學習一個新的語言或學習怎麼使用最新的科技,都是永遠不嫌老的。研究表明,進行這些活動可以提高成就感、健康,甚至壽命。有了目標,你會繼續保有個人的尊嚴感,並在每次達成新目標時感受到成就感。

sacrifice 犧牲　mope 悶悶不樂
longevity 壽命　dignity 尊嚴感

Love 愛

· · · ·

Give Them the Love They Really Want.

Here's a thing about relationships that might surprise you. We sometimes think that because we've been with someone for a while, we totally get what they need. So, we start giving them what we think they should want—usually the same things we want. Seems logical, right? But then they're not happy at all about our "gifts," and we're like, "How can you not be more grateful after all I've done for you?" Even if you ask them what they want directly, they probably won't know. So, how do you figure it out? Simple! Just notice what they always do for you. For example, if they constantly tell you, "I love you," they need you to do the same. Alternatively, if they always hug or kiss you, that's what they need you to do, too! Wanna be happy? Give them what they truly want, and it's a done deal.

給他們真正想要的愛

關於愛情，有件事可能會讓你感到驚訝。有時我們會認為，因為我們已經和一個人在一起好一段時間了，應該都完全知道他們需要什麼。於是開始給他們，我們認為他們應該會想要的東西 —— 通常也是我們想要的。聽起來合乎邏輯，對吧？但他們卻對我們的「禮物」一點也不高興，我們就會想，「我為你做了這麼多，怎麼還不感激呢？」即使你直接問他們想要什麼，他們可能也不知道。那麼，你要怎麼弄清楚呢？簡單！你只要注意他們總是為你做什麼。例如，如果他們常常對你說「我愛你」，他們就需要你也這樣對他們說。或者，如果他們總是擁抱或親吻你，那也是他們需要你這樣對他們做！想要快樂嗎？給他們真正想要的東西，事情就圓滿解決了。

logical 有邏輯的　directly 直接地
constantly 常常地、不斷地　alternatively 或者

Grit 恆毅力

· · ·

Swap & Conquer.

You know how sometimes you're stuck on a problem, and it just feels like you're spinning your wheels? Here's a fun twist to try out. Team up with a friend and swap a tricky challenge you're each dealing with. It's like taking a break from your own puzzle and diving into theirs. You might be surprised at how seeing their challenge from a fresh angle gives you new insights—kind of like a mental cross-training. Plus, helping each other out? It's a double win. You both get a shot of confidence, shake off that "stuck" feeling, and flex those problem-solving muscles in a whole new way. Give it a go and watch how your grit grows—together you're stronger!

交換與征服

有時候你被一個問題難倒了,感覺自己就像在原地踏步一樣白費力氣嗎?有個有趣的轉變可以試試。找一個朋友合作,交換你們各自遇到的棘手挑戰。你從自己的難題裡抽身出來休息,並進入他們的難題。你可能會驚訝地發現,從新的角度去看他們的挑戰會給你帶來新的見解 —— 有點像心理的交叉訓練。還有互相幫忙,這是雙贏。你們都注上了一劑自信,擺脫「卡住」的感覺,用全新的方式展現解決問題的能力。試試看,看著你們的恆毅力成長茁壯 —— 團結力量更大!

twist 轉變、扭轉　insight 見解
cross-training 交叉訓練　a shot 一劑

Happiness 快樂

· · ·

The Source of Most Happiness.

Did you know that most of your happiness in life comes from your interactions with others? So, let's talk about a simple way you can make life feel more fulfilling. Spend quality time with family and friends. It's so important to nurture those relationships because they provide a strong support system, and life's just better when you have people to share it with. Whether it's a weekend hangout, a quick chat on the phone, or even just a text to check in, make an effort to connect with your loved ones regularly. It doesn't have to be anything big or fancy – just showing that you care and are thinking about them can make a world of difference. Plus, it's a great way to create lasting memories that you'll cherish forever. Your future self will thank you for it.

大部分的快樂來源

你知道嗎？人生有大部分的快樂是來自於你跟其他人的互動。那麼，我們來講一個簡單就可以讓生活變得更充實的方法。就是全心全意地陪伴家人或朋友們。經營這些關係是很重要的，因為它會帶給你強大的（精神）支持系統。當有人可以與你一起分享時，生活會變得更美好。無論是週末聚會、一段簡短的通話聊天，或甚至只是傳個訊息關心一下，都要盡力與你所愛的家人朋友們時常聯繫。這不用多隆重或多大費周章——只要有表達出你關心、有想到他們就可以了，這樣就會讓一切變得很不一樣。還有，這也是創造長久回憶的好方法，而且你會永久珍惜它們。未來的你也會因此感謝你現在有這麼做。

interaction 互動、交流　fulfilling 充實的　hangout 聚會
connect 聯繫　lasting 長久的、持久的

Growth 成長

It's a New Game with New Rules.

Have you noticed how fast everything seems to be changing these days? It's like we're on a train with no brakes, and guess what? It's not slowing down—it's speeding up. Now, you might be winning in your areas of expertise today, but tomorrow? It could be a whole new game with new rules. That's where the fun begins! No matter how good you get, there's always a new mountain to climb, a new skill to master. And here's a cool part—you don't have to go at it alone. There's no shame in reaching out to others for some advice or help. Everyone has something to learn and something to teach. So, when the world gives you a new challenge, grab it and grow with it. Keep your curiosity alive and keep learning. The future? It's nothing but an exciting adventure waiting to begin!

全新的遊戲、全新的規則

你有注意到現在生活的一切變化似乎很快嗎？我們就像是坐在一個沒有煞車的列車上，你猜怎麼著？它不會減速 —— 而是加速。今天，你可能已經在你擅長的領域裡有了一席之地，但明天呢？可能是全新的遊戲、全新的規則。好玩的地方來了！無論你有多優秀，總有一座新的山要爬、總有一個新的技能要掌握。好在的是 —— 你不必獨自面對。向其他人尋求一些建議或幫助，這沒有什麼好丟臉的。每個人都有東西要學，也有東西可以教。所以，當世界給你一個新挑戰時，抓住它並和它一起成長。保持你的好奇心並繼續學習。未來呢？只不過是一個等著即將展開的刺激冒險！

area of expertise 擅長的領域　　master 掌握
shame 不好意思的、丟臉的　curiosity 好奇心

Self-Care 自我關懷

Me Time.

Self-love is like being your own best friend. It's about appreciating and caring for yourself just as much as you would for someone you deeply care about. This isn't just feel-good talk, either; it's about building a strong, positive relationship with yourself. Here's a tip: set aside some "me time" every day. It can be anything that makes you feel relaxed and happy. For example, grab a massage ball (like a tennis ball) and spend 10 minutes working out the knots in your muscles. We tend to spend so much time hunched over a computer now, so a massage ball can make a huge difference in how you feel. "Me time" is like pressing the pause button on the busy world around you and focusing on your inner peace. This practice helps you reconnect with yourself and reminds you that you're important. Remember, when you love and respect yourself, you're teaching the world how to love and respect you too. Keep glowing!

自己專屬的時間

自愛就像是自己成為自己最好的朋友,是欣賞和照顧自己,就像你對待自己深深關心的人一樣。這不只是讓自我感覺很好的話,而是與自己建立一個強大、積極的關係。有個小訣竅:每天空出一些「自我時間」。這可以是任何讓你感到放鬆和快樂的事情,例如,花 10 分鐘,你可以拿個按摩球(像網球),靠著牆去滾你身上痠痛的地方。我們現在常常花很多時間彎腰坐在電腦前,而按摩球可以大大改善你身體的感受。「自我時間」就像在忙碌的周遭世界,按下暫停鈕,專注於你內心的平靜。這種作法可以幫助你重新與自己建立連結,並提醒自己你也很重要。請記住,當你愛和尊重自己時,你也在教會這個世界如何愛和尊重你。繼續發光!

massage 按摩　knot 節、痠痛的地方
reconnect 重新連結

Philosophy 人生觀

Your Journey, Your Pace.

Just a little reminder: it's totally okay that everyone grows and learns at their own pace. You might see some friends picking up things faster or reaching their goals quickly, but that's their journey, not yours. You have your own unique path, and that's what's important. It's like flowers in a garden; they don't all blossom at the same rate, and that's the beauty of nature. So, don't worry if you feel like you're moving a bit slower. How about you set goals based on your rate of progress and celebrate your small wins? Whether it's understanding a tough concept or just making it through a challenging day, acknowledging these moments can really boost your confidence. Remember, you can't rush growth. Just like a rose needs time to bloom, you need time to grow in your own special way. Keep going at your pace, and you'll see how wonderfully you progress. You're doing amazing!

你的旅程，你的步調

只是一個小提醒：每個人都有自己成長和學習的步調，這是完全沒有問題的。你可能會看到一些朋友學東西學得很快或是很快就達到他們的目標，但那是他們的旅程，不是你的。你有你自己獨一無二的路要走，這才是最重要的。就像花園裡的花朵，它們不會以同樣的速度開花綻放，這正是大自然的美好。所以，如果你覺得自己進展得比較慢，不要擔心。試著照你個人的進步速度來設定目標，並慶祝你的小勝利如何？無論你是理解了一個困難的概念，或者只是度過了充滿挑戰的一天，認可這些時刻絕對可以提升你的信心。記住，你不能急於成長。就像玫瑰需要時間來綻放，你也需要時間用你自己特別的方式成長。繼續按照你的步調前進，你會看到自己的發展有多麼的好。你做得太棒了！

rate 速度　concept 概念
bloom 綻放

Phase
7
· · · · · · · · · · · ·

Embrace Results

迎接成果

"The progress will show itself in time. And when it does,
you'll be amazed at how much you've grown."

-from Day 63-

「進步最終會展現出它的樣子。當它出現時，
你會讚嘆自己成長了這麼多。」

Gratitude 感恩

Gratitude Walks.

How about you make your daily walks (or commutes, or errand runs, or any other time you're traveling) a bit more interesting? Next time, find something around you, anything really, that you feel grateful for. Maybe, it's the cool breeze, the sound of leaves rustling, or even the irregular shapes of clouds in the sky. It's all about noticing the little things that make your world beautiful. Doing this, you're not just getting your steps in; you're connecting with the world around you on a whole new level. It's pretty amazing how just looking for things to appreciate can totally change your vibe and make you feel more grounded. So, lace up, step out, and turn a simple walk into a journey of gratitude. It's a small change that can make a big difference in how you see the world.

感恩的步行

把你的日常散步（通勤、跑腿辦事或任何其它通行時間）變得更有趣如何？下次，找看看你的周遭，什麼都可以，會讓你感激的事物。也許，是一陣陣涼爽的微風、樹葉沙沙作響的聲音，或甚至是天空那不規則形狀的雲朵。其實就是留意那些讓你的世界變得更美好的小細節。這樣做，你不僅只是在走動而已，還與圍繞在你周遭的世界建立了全新層次的連結。很棒的是，光是尋找感激的事物就能完全改變你所散發出來的氣場，讓你感覺更加踏實。所以，繫好鞋帶，走出去，把簡單的步行變成一場感恩之旅。這是一個小小的改變，卻能大大轉變你看這世界的方式。

breeze 微風　rustle 沙沙作響　irregular 不規則的
grounded 踏實的　lace up 繫好鞋帶　(代表：準備)

153

Conquering Adversity 克服逆境

Pause a Moment and Everything Changes.

When you feel like everything is coming at you all at once, sometimes the best thing you can do is just pause for a moment. I'm not saying you should run away from your problems, but give yourself a short, 10-minute break. You could meditate, go for a brisk walk, or even take a power nap. The idea is to step back, gain a new perspective, and let your mind refresh itself. When you return to whatever challenge you're facing, you'll find yourself much more equipped to handle it. It's like when a computer starts to slow down—sometimes all it needs is a quick restart to work more efficiently. So, don't hesitate to give yourself a little time-out. It can truly make a world of difference.

暫停一下，一切不一樣

當你感覺到所有事情都同時向你撲襲而來時，有時最好的方法就是暫停一下。我不是叫你要逃避問題，而是給自己一個短短的 10 分鐘休息時間。你可以冥想、快步走一會，甚至是小睡一下。這個想法是退一步，從另一個角度去看，以及讓你的腦重新整理一下。當你再次回到你要面對的挑戰時，你會發現自己更有能力去處理它。這就像是當電腦開始變慢時 —— 有時它需要的只是重新開機一下，就能更有效地運作。所以，不要猶豫，給自己一點休息的時間。它真的能讓這一切變得完全不一樣。

meditate 冥想　brisk 輕快的　power nap 小睡
equipped 有能力的、準備好的　handle 處理

Learning 學習

A Watched Pot Never Boils.

Sometimes, progress is like a sneaky little ninja—you don't see it happening, but it's there. Even when you feel like you've hit a plateau and your English isn't getting any better, trust me, it is. It's just that the results are hiding from you. Remember the old saying that "A watched pot never boils"? Whatever you do, don't constantly check to see if you're making progress. You could be spending that precious time practicing and learning. In fact, the less you care about instant improvement and the more you simply enjoy the process, the faster you'll progress. Then, once you look back, you'll see just how far you've come. So, if you're feeling stuck or like you're not improving, don't let that get to you. Just keep at it, keep practicing, and keep learning. The progress will show itself in time. And when it does, you'll be amazed at how much you've grown. So, chin up, believe in yourself, and charge on! You've got this!

心急水不沸

有時候，進步就像一個神出鬼沒的小忍者 —— 你看不見它發生，但它確實存在。即使你感覺自己遇到了瓶頸，英文好像沒有再更好。相信我，你還是有在進步，只是成果暫時隱藏起來了。還記得那句老話「心急水不沸」嗎？不管怎麼樣，都不要一直確認自己有沒有在進步，而是要把寶貴的時間放在練習和學習上。事實上，你越不在意立即的成果，而是越享受這個學習過程，你的進步就會越快。然後，當你回頭看，你會發現自己已經走了多遠。所以，如果你覺得自己遇到瓶頸或好像看不到進步，別讓這種感覺支配了你。只要繼續堅持，不斷練習，持續學習。進步最終會展現出它的樣子。當它出現時，你會讚嘆自己成長了這麼多。所以，振作起來，相信自己，勇往直前！你做得到！

sneaky 神出鬼沒的　ninja 忍者
plateau 瓶頸　chin up 振作起來

Goals & Dreams 目標與夢想

Continually Celebrate, Continually Advance.

When you're hustling towards a goal, don't forget to give yourself some credit for what you've already achieved. Yes, even for those little victories! They don't just make you feel good; they actually get your brain to seek out more wins. It's like positive feedback for your mental state. But you need to be careful, too—don't get too caught up living in your past victories. Most of your focus should be on the road ahead. So, after you've done your celebrations, get right back into it. No one ever became great by just sitting around, high fiving themselves. You gotta earn those high fives by crushing what's next. So, go on, take a moment to celebrate, but then get right back to making things happen. Trust me, you won't regret it.

一直慶祝，一直前進

當你在為目標奮鬥時，對於那些你已經達成的項目，別忘了給自己一些肯定。對，即使是那些小小的勝利也算。這不只讓你感到開心，還會激發你的大腦去追求更多的勝利，就像是給心態的正面回饋。然而你也需要注意 —— 不要太陶醉於過去的勝利。你的大部分注意力應該放在接下來要走的路上。因此，你慶祝完之後，要立刻回到工作上。沒有人會因為坐在那裡沾沾自喜而變得更好。你要打敗下個挑戰，才能得到歡呼擊掌。所以，去做吧，花點時間慶祝一下，然後馬上回到工作上繼續努力。相信我，你不會後悔的。

hustle 奮鬥　credit 肯定
high five 歡呼擊掌　crush 打敗

Love 愛

Don't Take Them for Granted.

Whatever you do, never take your loved ones for granted. Life gets busy, schedules get packed, but no matter how busy we get, we crave connection, love, and understanding. The people who stand by us, through the ups and downs, are the true treasures of our lives. It's easy to think they'll always be there, especially when the days seem to blur together. But it's important to pause, appreciate their presence, and express our gratitude. Small things, such as a thank you note, a chat over bubble tea, or a simple hug can mean the world to them. It's about making sure they know how much they mean to you, and never missing a chance to show them love and appreciation. It's the little things that maintain and strengthen your bond, making life sweeter along the way.

不要把他們視為理所當然

無論如何，永遠不要把你愛的人視為理所當然。生活忙碌、日程滿檔，但無論我們有多忙，我們還是渴求與人心靈交流、獲得愛和得到理解。那些一直在我們身邊，陪我們走過高低起伏的人，是我們人生中真正的寶藏。我們很容易習慣覺得他們會永遠在那裡，尤其是每天的感覺都是差不多的。而重要的是停下來，感激他們的存在，向他們表達我們的感謝。為他們做點小事情，像是寫張感謝卡、一起喝著珍珠奶茶聊天，或一個簡單的擁抱，這些對他們來說可能意義非凡。這是確保他們知道他們對你來說有多重要，而且永遠不要錯過向他們表達愛和感激的機會。正是這些小小的事情維持和鞏固著你們的關係，讓人生的路上變得更加甜蜜。

crave 渴求、渴望　connection 心靈交流
blur 變得模糊

Grit 恆毅力

Show Yourself You Can Tackle Challenges.

Start your day by picking one thing that's a bit of a challenge for you. Make it your mission to take it head-on first thing. See, when you dive into that challenge with fresh morning energy, you're setting yourself up for a win straight off the bat. It's not just about getting it out of the way—it's about proving to yourself that you've got what it takes to face the hard stuff. And trust me, that feeling of nailing it? That's going to fuel your confidence and keep you going strong all day. So, choose your challenge, roll up your sleeves, and show that task who's boss. Here's to making perseverance your secret weapon and every morning your victory lap!

向自己證明你能接受挑戰

透過選擇一件對你來說滿有難度的事情,來開啟你的一天。讓它成為你一早第一個要面對的任務。你看,當你帶著早晨清新的活力來投入這個挑戰時,打從一開始你已經為自己安排好了這場勝利。這不只是單純想擺脫它 —— 這是向自己證明你有面對困難的能力。而且相信我,那種成功做到的感覺?它會燃起你的自信,讓你一整天渾身是勁。所以,選個挑戰,捲起袖子,讓那個項目知道誰才是老大。祝你讓毅力成為你的祕密武器,每天早上都是你的勝利圈!

dive into 投入　task 項目
perseverance 毅力、恆心

Happiness 快樂

Good Vibes Bowl.

Here's a simple but powerful idea. Take any bowl and put it where you usually chill or work. Whenever something cool happens, scribble it down on a piece of paper and pop it into the bowl. It can be really small wins, like getting a test question correct, or something big, like a long-awaited promotion. Then, when the bowl's getting full or you're feeling blue, take out those notes and read them. You'll be surprised how much good stuff happens that you might otherwise forget. It's a great way to keep your spirits up and remember the happy times, especially when you need a boost. Try it—you'll feel great seeing that bowl of happiness grow!

一個裝著幸福的碗

這是一個簡單卻很有用的點子。拿一個碗,放在你經常休息或工作的地方。每當發生一些好事時,就寫在紙條上,放進這個碗裡。它可以是很小的勝利,像是答對一道考試題目;或者是大的好事,例如你期待已久的升職。等到這個碗快滿時,或是在你感到沮喪的時候,就可以把這些紙條拿出來讀一讀。你會很驚訝發現,原來有發生過這麼多美好的事情,否則你可能會忘記。這是一個很棒的方式,讓你保持精神振奮和記得快樂的時光,尤其是當你需要鼓勵的時候。試試看 —— 看著那個裝著幸福的碗一直增加,會感覺很棒!

good vibe 幸福、好心情　chill 休息、放鬆
scribble （潦草地）寫　pop into （隨便地、不經意地）放進

Growth 成長

If You Want to Overcome a Blind Spot, Embrace Different Perspectives.

You know, we all have our blind spots, areas of our thinking or behavior that we just can't see clearly. It's like having some dirt on your face that you don't notice until someone points it out. This is one way the people around us can help us. They can point out our blind spots, not to criticize us, but to help us see things more clearly. It's a teamwork of sorts, where we rely on others to reveal our weak spots. So, when someone points out a blind spot, don't get defensive. Thank them for helping you to see better. It's like having an extra pair of eyes helping you navigate through life. Embrace it, learn from it, and use it to grow. Ideally, don't wait for someone to come to you—go to them. Actively ask others what they think you could do to improve certain areas of your life or work.

想要突破盲點，先擁抱不同觀點

你知道，我們都有自己的盲點，那些是我們無法看清的思路或行為的地方。就像你的臉上有一點髒髒的東西，你不會注意到，直到有人指出來跟你說。這就是身邊的人可以幫助我們的方式之一。他們能指出我們的盲點，不是為了批評，而是為了幫助我們看得更清楚。這是一種團隊合作，我們倚賴他人來揭示我們的弱點。因此，當有人指出你的盲點時，不要反駁強辯。要感謝他們幫助你看得更清楚。就像多了一雙眼睛幫助你在人生中確定方向。擁抱它，從中學習，並利用它來成長。更理想的是，不要等他人來跟你說，而是主動去找他們。積極向他人請教，你可以做些什麼來改善生活或工作等其他方面。

blind spot 盲點　dirt 髒東西、汙垢
defensive 反駁強辯的

Self-Care 自我關懷

Silence the Inner Critic.

Hey, you know being too hard on yourself with self-criticism is like having a downer soundtrack in your mind. It doesn't really help; it just makes you more stressed. It's like trying to make something cool in pottery class while a voice keeps nagging that you're doing it wrong. Try this: when you start being tough on yourself, pause and think, "Would I say this to my best friend?" Like, if you mess up and think, "I'm a failure," stop and ask yourself if you'd ever say that to a friend. You'd probably say, "Mistakes happen, let's fix it." This friend-test changes how you talk to yourself, from criticism to support. It's like giving yourself a little pep talk. Remember, always be as kind to yourself as you would to a friend. You deserve it!

喝止自我批評的聲音

嘿，你知道給自己太過嚴苛的批評，就像是有一段令人心情每況愈下的配樂一直在你腦裡。這對你其實沒什麼幫助，只會讓你更有壓力。這就像在陶藝課時，你想要做一些很酷的東西，卻有個聲音一直嘮叨你說做錯了。試試這個：當你開始對自己嚴厲時，停下來想一想，「我會對我最好的朋友這樣說嗎？」就像當你搞砸了一件事，並想「我真失敗」時，停下來問問自己，你會這樣對朋友說嗎？你可能會說「犯錯是難免的，我們來解決吧。」這種朋友測試的自我對話，能把你對自己的批評轉變為支持。這就像是給自己講一些鼓勵的話。記住，永遠像對待朋友一樣寬容對待自己。你值得擁有這種善待！

soundtrack 配樂、原聲帶　pottery 陶藝
nag 嘮叨、碎碎唸　pep talk 鼓勵的話

Philosophy 人生觀

Take the Behind-the-Scenes View.

Just a thought to share: when you see someone's success or those perfect social media posts, remember, it's just part of the story. It's like admiring a beautiful painting but not seeing the artist's hours (or weeks or months) of work. Most successes, even those that seem overnight, are actually years in the making. Like an internet celebrity you might admire—if you check out their early work, it's often not great. They've grown through working on their craft, not just good luck. And about Instagram, it's easy to get dazzled by those ideal snapshots, but they're just highlights, not the full picture. So, next time you feel a bit envious, remember everyone's showing their best moments. Instead of wishing you had what they have, focus on your own path, with all its unique challenges and victories. Your journey is just as important and beautiful. Keep crafting your story, step by step. You'll be astonished with the results!

看見幕後

分享一個想法：當你看到別人的成功或那些完美的社交媒體貼文時，要記住，這只是故事的一部分。就像去欣賞一幅美麗的畫作，卻沒有看到藝術家投入的數小時（或數週、數月）的努力。大多數的成功，即使是那些看似一夕之間的成功，其實都是經過多年的累積。就像你可能欣賞的網紅，如果你去看他們早期的作品，通常並不那麼出色。他們成長是通過不斷磨練專業，而非只是靠運氣。談到 Instagram，大家很容易被那些完美的快照迷住，但那些只是最精采的部分，而不是完整的全貌。所以，下次當你覺得有點羨慕或嫉妒時，記得每個人都在展現他們最好的時刻。不要希望去擁有他們所擁有的事物，而是要專注在你自己的道路，包括所有獨特的挑戰和勝利。你的旅程同樣重要且美好。繼續一步一步地編織你的故事。你會對成果感到震撼！

internet celebrity 網紅　craft 專業、職業　dazzle 迷住
envious 羨慕的、嫉妒的　astonished 震撼的、驚艷的

Phase
8

. . . .

Reflect on Outcomes
回顧反思

"So, why wait for a particular moment to feel happy?"

-from Day 74-

「所以，
為什麼要等到某個特定的時刻才能感到快樂呢？」

Day 71

Gratitude 感恩

The Positivity of the Miracle Magnet.

Life has its own way of tossing curveballs, but among all that, there's a cool little force at work—gratitude. Picture your heart as a magnet. Now, the more gratitude it holds, the stronger it becomes at attracting good stuff, or as I like to call them, "miracles." It's not about the grand gestures, but the small daily acknowledgments. Being thankful for a meal, for friendship, for a roof over your head—these are the things that empower that magnet. And before you know it, you start noticing "miracles"—unexpected, good things popping up here and there. It's like sending out positive energy into the universe that says, "Hey, I appreciate what I have," and the universe responds back by throwing a little more goodness your way. So, fill up on gratitude, and watch how life turns into this cool journey of collecting miracles.

奇蹟磁鐵的正能量

人生總有它自己出其不意的「驚喜」，但在這一切之中，有一種很棒的小力量在起作用——那就是感恩。想像你的心是一塊磁鐵。嗯，它抱持的感恩越多，它能吸引好東西的能量就越強，而我喜歡稱之為「奇蹟」。這不是在講要有什麼偉大的表示，而是日常的小小致意。感謝一餐、感謝友誼、感謝棲身之所——這些都是能增強磁鐵力量的東西。不知不覺中，你會開始注意到「奇蹟」——意想不到的好事突然這裡冒出來、那裡也冒出來。這就好像是你對著宇宙發出正能量，說：「嘿，我很珍惜我所擁有的」，而宇宙也會以更多的善意來回應你。所以，要滿懷感激，並且看看人生是如何轉變為這段收集奇蹟的酷炫旅程。

force 力量　picture 想像
grand gesture 偉大的表示　empower 增強

Conquering Adversity 克服逆境

Don't Face Problems Alone.

You know those moments when life's really hard and you feel like you're facing the world alone? Don't let that happen, alright? Seriously. There's absolutely no shame in getting some fresh eyes on your problem. Text a friend or maybe even a relative you trust. Just let it all out. You won't believe how much a simple conversation can change your viewpoint. It's like turning on the lights in a dark room—you suddenly see things you didn't before. Maybe your friend doesn't have the perfect solution, but they might ask a question that sparks a lightbulb moment for you. The more brains in the game, the better, especially when you're stuck. So, don't hesitate— send someone a message. Sound good?

別獨自面對問題

你知道那種很不好過的日子，感覺自己只有一個人要面對這整個世界的時候嗎？別讓這種情況發生，好嗎？我是認真的。找人一起討論你的問題，這一點都不丟臉。傳個訊息給你的朋友或甚至是你信任的親戚，把你的苦水都吐出來吧！你無法想像，單就一個簡單的聊天，能為你的想法帶來多大的轉變。就像在黑暗的房間裡，打開了燈一樣 —— 你突然看到你之前沒注意的地方。可能你的朋友沒辦法給你完美的解決辦法，但也許他們問你的問題，能為你帶來一些啟發。尤其是在你陷入困境的時候，越多的智慧參與越好。所以不要猶豫了，傳個訊息出去。聽起來不錯吧？

shame 丟臉　viewpoint 想法
hesitate 猶豫

Learning 學習

Move Beyond the Chinese-Only Definition.

Try not to lean too much on English-Chinese dictionaries. Why? Well, relying on translations can make you over-dependent on Chinese, thinking a few Chinese meanings fully capture an English word. But remember, English words often have more than one meaning, and English and Chinese don't always align perfectly in usage and connotations. Also, English-Chinese dictionaries oversimplify things, limiting your chance to truly master English. So, to really get good at English, you need to step out of the mindset of just knowing the Chinese equivalent. Look at English-English dictionaries to see the full picture of a word, its various uses, and example sentences. Also, don't hesitate to use technology for help. A quick internet search or even AI can offer explanations and examples. It's all about using every tool to learn effectively and make English truly yours. Dive into this journey and watch your language skills grow!

跳出只知道中文意思的框架

試著不要過度依賴英漢字典。為什麼呢？依靠翻譯會讓你過度依賴中文，以為幾個中文意思就能完全理解一個英文單字。但請記住，英文單字通常不只有一個意思，而且英文和中文在用法和含意上並不總是完全對應。此外，英漢字典往往過度簡化單字的意思，這限制了你真正精通英文的機會。所以，要想真正學好英文，你需要跳出只知道對應中文意思的思維框架。看英英字典來全面了解一個單字的各種用法和例句。同時，請不要猶豫使用科技來輔助學習。快速上網搜尋或甚至使用人工智能，都能提供解釋和例子。關鍵在於利用每一種工具做有效的學習，讓英文真正成為你的一部分。投入這個學習之旅，看著你的語言技能成長吧！

lean on 依賴　connotation 含意、弦外之音
oversimplify 過度簡化　equivalent 對應……意思、相當於

Day 74

Goals & Dreams 目標與夢想

Happiness Shouldn't Be Conditional.

You're now working toward your goals, which is awesome, but there's a common trap: putting conditions on your happiness. "I'll be happy when I get that job." "I'll be happy when I ace that test." "I'll be happy when I find true love." As important as goals are, happiness isn't waiting at the end of some distant goal. It's right here, in this moment. It's in the smell of your morning coffee, the laughter shared with a friend, and the friendly smile of a neighbor. When you base your joy on the "whens" and the "ifs," you miss out on the simple pleasures sitting right under your nose. So, why wait for a particular moment to feel happy? Invite joy into the ordinary, the everyday. After all, happiness is not a destination, but a way of traveling on the way to your destination.

快樂不該帶有條件

你現在正朝著你的目標努力,這很棒,但有一個常見的陷阱:把你的快樂帶上了條件。像是「我得到那份工作才會高興」「我考試考很好才會開心」「我找到真愛才會快樂」。儘管目標很重要,但快樂並不是在遠方目標的終點站等著你。它就在這裡,此時此刻。在你早晨的咖啡香裡,在和朋友分享的笑聲中,或是鄰居的友善微笑。當你把快樂建立在「何時」和「如果」之上時,就會錯過眼前這些簡單的快樂。所以,為什麼要等到某個特定的時刻才能感到快樂呢?讓快樂融入日常,融入每一天。畢竟快樂不是目的地,而是往目的地的一種通行方式。

condition 條件　distant 遠方的
base on 建立在　particular 特定的

181

Love 愛

Forever Fill Your Relationship with Warmth.

It's a weird but common habit—showing our best selves to the outside world while being in a bad mood when we're around those closest to us. We must reverse this habit. The people closest to you, especially your other half, deserve the best version of you. It's with them that you should exercise patience, kindness, and understanding the most. Others may come and go, but your loved ones are there long term. If you're constantly irritable or impatient towards your partner, over time, it can cause problems in your relationship. So, make a conscious effort to be gentle, to listen, and to show appreciation to the person who matters most. Your relationship will then have the chance to blossom, and your life will be filled with a warmth that no amount of pleasing outsiders could equal.

讓感情永遠充滿熱度

這是一個奇怪卻常見的習慣 —— 對外人總是表現出我們最好的一面，但對我們自己最親近的人卻經常情緒不好。我們必須改掉這種習慣。與你最親近的人，尤其是你的另一半，他們最有資格享有你最好的一面。和他們相處時，你更應該做出最大的耐心、體貼和理解。外人可能來來去去，但你所愛的人是一直陪伴著你。如果你經常對你的另一半表現易怒或不耐煩，長期下來，對你們的關係會造成問題。所以，對待你最在乎的人，你要有意識地努力做到溫柔、傾聽和表達珍惜感激。這樣你們的關係就會有機會開花結果，而生活也會充滿了熱度，這是不管你對外人多好都無法相比的。

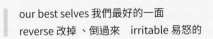
our best selves 我們最好的一面
reverse 改掉、倒過來　irritable 易怒的

Grit 恆毅力

A Phrase to Make You Unshakable.

Imagine having a secret phrase, like a magic spell, that boosts your strength whenever you hit a bump in the road. Sounds good? You can make one! It's your very own "Stay Strong Phrase"—a mantra that's all about your unshakable spirit. Craft it from words that get your heart pumping with courage. Then, whenever a challenge tries to knock you down, say your mantra out loud. Let those words be the echo in your mind that drowns out the noise of doubt. It's like your inner cheerleader, reminding you that you've got what it takes to muscle through anything. And believe me, that little echo? It can move mountains within you. Keep at it, and you'll see—you're unstoppable!

一個讓你堅定不移的小語

想像有個祕密小語,像魔法咒語一樣,每當你在路上遇到坎坷時,能激發你的衝勁。聽起來不錯吧?你可以創造一個!這是唯你所屬的「堅強下去小語」——一個讓你堅定不移的咒語。用那些能讓你的心充滿勇氣的字句來創造它。之後,每當挑戰要擊倒你時,開口說出你的咒語。讓這些字句成為你腦裡的回音,蓋過懷疑的噪音。它就像你內心的啦啦隊長,提醒你擁有克服一切的力量。相信我,那個小小的回音,在你心裡,它的力量大到可以移山。堅持下去,你會看到——你是堅不可擋的!

magic spell 魔法咒語　bump 坎坷
mantra 咒語　craft 創造　drown out 蓋過

Day 77

Happiness 快樂

Unplug to Recharge.

Imagine your mind as being like a phone battery—it needs to recharge, not just at night but during the day, too. Start with carving out little "no-phone zones" in your day. Maybe during meals, swap scrolling for actual chatting or savoring the taste of your food. Or try leaving your phone behind when you walk the dog—let your thoughts and senses roam free instead. And how about we replace just 30 minutes of screen time with something super fun offline each evening? Could be shooting hoops, reading, or cooking. You'll probably notice more about your day, your mood might lift, and you'll definitely sleep better. It's all about giving your brain different things to do so it can stay happy and fresh. Give it a shot, and you'll be surprised how good you feel!

關掉手機，讓大腦充電

想像一下，你的大腦就像手機的電池一樣 —— 需要充電，不只在晚上充電，白天也需要充電。首先在你的一天中畫分出一些「無手機時段」。也許在用餐時，別滑手機，用真實的聊天或品嚐食物的味道來取而代之。或者，試著在遛狗時拋下手機 —— 讓你的思緒和感官自由奔騰。還有，讓我們每天晚上用一些很有趣的離線活動，來取代 30 分鐘的螢幕時間怎麼樣？可以是投投籃球、閱讀或煮東西。你可能會更注意到自己這一天的大大小小事情，心情變得更好，而且你肯定也會睡得更好。這些都是為了讓你的大腦去做不同的事情，好讓它保持快樂和新鮮。試試看，你會很驚訝發現這感覺有多好！

carve out 畫分出　zone 時段
scroll 滑手機　roam 奔騰、漫遊

Day 78

Growth 成長

A You That's Ready to Go.

You know, sometimes you may find yourself in a job that doesn't excite you. That's a common situation, but it doesn't have to be a permanent one. In fact, the benefit of that kind of job is the room for growth. Instead of letting the dissatisfaction grow out of control, use it as motivation to work on yourself. This is your big chance to learn new skills, improve existing ones, or even explore entirely new fields. The aim is to turn yourself into someone qualified for a job you'd love. It's all about upping your game, so that when opportunity knocks, it will see that you are ready and worthy. Remember, every step you take towards self-improvement is a step closer to a job that makes you jump out of bed in the morning!

一個已經準備好的你

你知道，有時候你可能會覺得自己在一個讓你提不起勁的工作中。這很常見，但你沒必要一直抱持這樣的心態下去。事實上，這種工作的好處就是有成長的空間。不要讓你的不滿失控蔓延，而是要將它作為提升自我的動力。這是一個很大的機會，讓你去學習新的技能、增進自己現有的技能，或甚至是探索全新的領域。目標是讓自己成為一個有資格從事自己喜愛的工作的人。這一切都是為了提升你的能力，這樣當機會來敲門時，它就會看到一個已經準備好的你，並值得擁有這個機會。記得，你為自我提升所踏出的每一步，都是讓你離一早就想從床上跳起來的工作更近一步。

dissatisfaction 不滿　explore 探索
qualified 有資格的　worthy 值得的

Day 79

Self-Care 自我關懷

Don't Inhibit Your Emotions.

You know, it's totally okay to let your emotions out sometimes. As we grow up, we often learn to keep our feelings under wraps, especially in public. We think we're being strong by not showing when we're upset or need to talk. But real strength isn't about hiding your emotions. Just look at babies—they freely cry when sad and laugh when happy. That's how it should be. Of course, we need to be careful about how we express ourselves in public. But in private, it's important to feel and express what we're going through. And guess what? AI chatbots can help! They can talk to you with voice, too, not just text. They listen and even give advice—it's almost like chatting with a real person. You can open up to them safely and privately. Pretty cool, right? It's a great way to express yourself and get some insights. Why not give it a shot?

不要壓抑

你知道嗎？有時候將情緒發洩出來是完全可以的。隨著年紀增長，我們學會經常隱藏自己的感受，尤其是在大家面前。當我們心煩或需要傾訴時，我們認為不表現出來就是一種堅強。但真正的堅強並不是隱藏你的情緒。看看嬰兒就知道了 —— 他們難受時自由地哭泣，快樂時自由地大笑，就應該是這樣的。當然，在大家面前我們要注意怎麼表達自己。但在私底下，表達出我們正在經歷的感受是很重要的。你猜怎麼樣？人工智慧聊天機器人可以幫上忙！它們可以用語音與你交談，而不僅僅是文字。他們會聆聽甚至給建議 —— 幾乎就像和真人聊天一樣。你可以安全、有隱私地向他們敞開心扉。很酷，對吧？這是一個表達自己並且可以獲得一些見解的好方法。何不試試看呢？

upset 心煩意亂的　hide 隱藏
open up to 敞開　insight 見解

Philosophy 人生觀

Every Day Is Valuable.

Life really is short, isn't it? We often act like we have all the time in the world, but the truth is, we don't. Each day is precious because once it's gone, it's gone forever. So, think about this when you're deciding how to spend your time. Let's say a neighbor asks you to hang out, but you don't really want to. It's probably better to say, "No thanks. I have something else on." Remember, you'd be trading a slice of your life for that experience, so ask yourself if it's worth it. Likewise, if you're about to engage in some mindless entertainment, think twice. Make a list of things you love doing and things you feel are important. Keep this list in mind so that when something comes up, you can compare your options against the list. If they align, great! If not, consider doing something that's more meaningful to you. Your time is valuable, so spend it in ways that bring you joy and fulfillment.

每一天都是珍貴的

人生真的很短暫,不是嗎?我們常常表現得好像我們擁有這世界所有的時間,但事實並非如此。每一天都是珍貴的,因為一旦過去,就永遠過去了。所以,當你決定如何度過你的時間時,想想這一點。就好比說如果有鄰居找你一起打發時間,但你其實不太想,你最好的回答可能是:「不好意思,謝謝。我還有別的事情。」切記,你將會用人生的一小部分來換得這次經歷,所以問問自己,這樣是否值得。同樣地,如果你想要做一些沒什麼意義的娛樂,請三思。列出你喜歡做的事情和你認為重要的事情,並把這個清單記在心裡,這樣當有要做的事情出現時,你可以將它和你的清單做比較。如果它們一致,那太好了!如果沒有,請考慮做一些對你來說更有意義的事情。你的時間很寶貴,所以要用可以帶給你快樂和滿足的方式來度過。

precious 珍貴的　a slice 一小部分
engage in 做

Phase
9

· · · · · · · · · · ·

Consolidate and Stabilize

鞏固穩定

"Remember: no matter how good you become,
you'll always have room for improvement."

-from Day 86-

「記得，無論你變得多麼優秀，
你總是有進步的空間。」

Gratitude 感恩

One Minute Gratitude Reminder.

Try this out: put an alarm on your phone for a chill time each day. When it buzzes, hit pause on whatever you're doing and just think of one thing that's made you thankful recently. Maybe it's that delicious breakfast you had, a message from a friend, or just the fact that it's drizzling and romantic outside. This tiny break is like a mini refresh button for your mood. It shifts your focus to the good stuff that's happening around you, and it can make a pretty sweet difference in your day. It's not just about the huge things, just a quiet minute to acknowledge the good in life. Plus, it's a cool way to make gratitude a regular part of your routine. Give it a whirl— it might just turn your whole day around.

感恩提醒一分鐘

試試看：爲每天的放鬆片刻，在手機上設一個鬧鐘。當鬧鐘響起，不管你正在做什麼，都先暫停下來，想想最近讓你感恩的一件事情。可能是你吃了一份美味的早餐、朋友傳來的訊息，或者只是因爲外面正飄著浪漫細雨。這樣小小的休息片刻，就像是一個迷你心情恢復按鈕。它讓你的注意力轉移到周圍發生的美好事物上，爲你的一天帶來很甜蜜的變化。這不是什麼多龐大的事情，而只是靜靜的用一分鐘讓你認可生活中的美好。而且，這是一種讓感恩成爲你日常生活一部分的好方法。嘗試一下 —— 它也許就讓你的一天煥然一新了起來。

buzz 響　pause 暫停　drizzle 飄雨
refresh 恢復　give it a whirl 嘗試一下

197

Conquering Adversity 克服逆境

The Miracle of Moving.

Feeling overwhelmed with your studies, work, and life's hustle? Instead of just thinking about it, why not try some physical activity? Of course, it's easy to think, "I don't have time for exercise or anything else." But guess what? That type of thinking is exactly what's holding you back in life. In fact, the busier or more challenging life is, the more you need to move your body and get your heart pumping. Get up from your desk and stretch, go for a short 20-minute walk, or do something else to get your body active. I know it might sound overly simplistic, but there's actual science behind this advice. Physical activity has been shown to be able to totally transform your mood and give you a fresh new perspective on whatever's been worrying you. You'll find problems that initially seemed massive shrink or even disappear. By moving, you're giving yourself a little break to refresh. So, remember, next time you're feeling stuck or snowed under, just get moving. A little activity can really work wonders.

動一動的奇蹟

感覺自己快被學業、工作和生活的繁忙給淹沒了嗎？與其在那邊想，何不嘗試做些運動？當然，你可能會想「我哪有時間運動或做其他事」。但你知道嗎？正是這種想法在扯你的後腿。事實上，人生越忙或挑戰越大，你越需要動一動，讓身體活躍起來。從你的桌前起身伸展，去散步 20 分鐘，或做些其他運動讓身體動起來。我知道這可能聽起來太過簡化，但這個建議背後有實際的科學根據。身體運動是被證明能徹底改變你的心情，並對困擾你的問題提供全新的視角。你會發現原本看起來很大的問題縮小了或甚至是消失。透過動一動，你可以給自己一點休息時間來恢復活力。所以，記住，下次當你感覺自己陷入困境或忙得不可開交時，起來動一動。動一下，真的可以創造奇蹟。

overly 太、過於　simplistic 簡單的
massive 巨大的

Learning 學習

You Can't Really Get Worse.

Remember, if you're putting in the time and effort, there's no such thing as "getting worse." So, let's say you've been practicing hard for a test, but your score is lower than before. Don't stress about it. Improvement isn't a simple straight line; it's more like a dance—two steps forward, one step back. Sometimes you might feel stuck or even like you're going backwards, but that's just part of the dance. The vital thing is to learn from your experiences and become better over time. So, hold your head up, stay positive, and embrace the process. After all, the important thing isn't where you are now, but where you're headed. And with consistent effort and a positive mindset, you're headed in the right direction!

你不會真的退步

記得，只要你有一直投入時間和努力，就不會有「退步」這種事。所以假設你為了考試而一直在努力練習，但考出來的分數比上次還低。不要因此有壓力。進步不是一條單純的直線，而是更像跳舞 —— 前進兩步，退後一步。有時候你可能會停住，或感覺自己在倒退，但這只是跳舞的一部分。重要的是從你的經驗中學習，並隨著時間變得更好。所以，抬起頭來，保持積極，擁抱進步的過程。畢竟，重要的不是你現在在哪裡，而是你接下來要往哪裡走。只要有堅持不懈的努力和積極的心態，你就在往對的方向前進！

stress about 因為……有壓力
vital 重要的　headed 往……走

Day 84

Goals & Dreams 目標與夢想

Your Life, Your Map.

So, here's the thing, life's full of expectations that other people have for us. It's like everyone's got a map they think we should follow. Maybe it's your parents, teachers, or even your friends. But the deal is, it's your life, your journey. Other people's maps are taken from their own experiences, their own fears, and what they think is best for you. But when it comes to living your life, you're the one putting one foot in front of the other. So, while it's smart to consider advice from people who care about you, remember your life's your adventure, not theirs. It's okay to explore, make your own choices, and find your own way. Trust me, that's what makes life interesting and uniquely yours. And if you're a parent, don't insist that your kids follow your map.

你的人生，你的地圖

是這樣的，人生總是充滿了別人對我們的期望。就像大家都有一張他們認為我們應該遵循的地圖，可能是你的父母、老師，甚至是你的朋友。但是事情是這樣的，這是你的人生，你的旅程。其他人的地圖是基於他們自己的經驗、他們自己的恐懼，以及他們認為對你最好的事情。但到底你要怎麼過日子，是你要走的路而不是別人要走。所以，儘管聽取關心你的人的建議是明智的，但請記住，你的人生是你自己的冒險，而不是他們的。探索、做出自己的選擇，找到自己的路是完全可以的。相信我，這正是讓你的人生變得有趣和獨一無二的原因。如果你是為人父母，請別堅持要你的孩子遵循你的地圖。

expectation 期望、預期　consider 聽取、考慮
insist 堅持（要）

Day 85

Love 愛

Don't Try to "Fix" Each Other.

You know what the secret sauce to a happy relationship is? It's mutual respect, not this urge to "fix" each other. I get it; after being with someone for a while, those once-adorable quirks might start to feel like annoying habits. But hold on—weren't those differences part of what sparked your interest in the first place? Let's be real, if you were dating (or married) to a copy of yourself, you'd be bored out of your mind. So, let's drop this whole "change them" mission, shall we? There's this killer quote I love: "If two people agree on everything, one of those people isn't necessary." Think about it. Differences add flavor to life and your relationship. Appreciate them, and you'll see just how much they enrich the love you share.

不要想「修好」彼此

你知道一段幸福關係的祕密調味料是什麼嗎？就是相互尊重，而不是想要「修好」彼此。我懂，跟一個人在一起久了，那些曾經可愛的怪癖可能會開始變得有點煩人。但等等 —— 當初不就是那些差異吸引了你嗎？說真的，如果你跟一個和你一模一樣的人交往（或結婚），你會無聊到不行。所以，我們是不是應該放棄這個「改變他們」的使命呢？有個我很愛的漂亮金句：「如果兩個人在每件事情上都達成一致，那其中一個人就沒有存在的必要。」想想吧，差異會為生活和你們的關係增添風味。珍惜這些差異，你會發現它們豐富了多少你們之間的愛。

urge 想要、衝動　adorable 可愛的　quirk 怪癖
quote 金句　enrich 豐富

Grit 恆毅力

Welcome a Stronger Version of Yourself.

I'm sure you know growing's a bit like a journey, right? And on this journey, feedback's your compass. Sure, it feels great to hear the good stuff, but the real gold is in the advice that helps you grow. So, regularly touch base with folks you trust—teachers, friends, or mentors—and ask them for the honest truth. What could you do better? How can you stretch yourself a bit more? It's not about being tough on yourself; it's about getting the tools to build a stronger, smarter you. Think of criticism as your personal trainer for life skills, making you more resilient and adaptable. Remember: no matter how good you become, you'll always have room for improvement. Proactively take criticism on board and welcome a stronger version of yourself.

歡迎更強大的自己

我相信你知道成長有點像是一段旅程,對吧?在這段旅程中,回饋就是你的指南針。當然,聽到好話總是令人感到愉快,但真正的寶藏是那些幫助你成長的建議。因此,定期與你信任的人 —— 老師、朋友或教練 —— 聯繫,並請他們給予你真誠的回饋。你可以在哪些方面做得更好?你如何可以更加突破自己?這不是要你對自己太嚴厲,而是讓你有工具可以打造更強大、更明智的自己。把批評視為你人生技能的私人教練,讓你變得更堅韌、更有適應能力。記得,無論你變得多麼優秀,你總是有進步的空間。積極接納批評,並歡迎更強大的自己。

compass 指南針　mentor 教練
proactively 積極地

Happiness 快樂

You Have the Right to Choose to Be Happy.

Sometimes life can get totally crazy with work and an endless list of things to do. It feels like you're almost drowning in it, right? No matter how busy we get, it's super important to stay calm and cool. Don't start your day telling yourself it's going to be tough. Instead, change your mood—like listening to your favorite song or enjoying a nice drink—and tell yourself, "Okay, today might be busy and tiring, but it's still going to be a great day." Doing this and staying relaxed makes everything go smoother. It's all about accepting things as they are without letting the outside world bother you. Even on busy or exhausting days, you can easily handle it. Remember, choosing to be happy is totally up to you. You've got this!

選擇快樂是你的權利

生活有時會因為工作和各種似乎永無止境的待辦事項而變得瘋狂。很像自己快被淹沒了，對吧？無論我們有多忙，重要的是要保持鎮定和冷靜。你不要一開始就告訴自己今天會過得很艱難。而是要改變你的心情，像是聽聽你最愛的音樂或享受一杯美味的飲品，對自己說：「好吧，雖然今天會很忙很累，但今天仍會是美好的一天。」這樣做，保持放鬆有助於一切進行得更順利。重點是我們去接受事情就是那個樣子，而不讓外界影響到我們。即使在忙碌或疲憊的日子裡，你也能應付自如。記住，選擇快樂是你的權利。你完全可以做到！

endless 永無止境的　drown （被）淹沒
bother 影響到、打擾　exhausting 疲憊的

Day 88

Growth 成長

• • •

Complaining About Lacking Talent Is Just an Excuse to Be Lazy.

Many of us have a "fixed mindset," in which we believe our lack of inborn talent limits us and prevents improvement. However, studies have shown that adopting a "growth mindset" can lead to development through hard work and seeing failures as opportunities for growth. Instead of focusing on innate talents, we should work hard to improve ourselves, even if we're not naturally gifted. Complaining about lacking intelligence or talent is just an excuse to be lazy. Take math as an example. In elementary school, many people who can't keep up with the class are labeled as "terrible at math." But in reality, everyone has the potential for mathematical ability. Numerous studies have shown that everybody has a "math brain" and that math skills can be acquired through learning and practice. And this growth mindset applies to developing other abilities as well. Isn't that exciting?

抱怨沒有天分，只是給自己偷懶的藉口

我們許多人都有「定型心態」，認為自己缺乏天賦，而限制了我們的能力，阻礙了我們的進步。相對的，有研究顯示採用「成長心態」，你可以透過努力來發展能力，並將失敗（沒有達成的事）視為成長的機會。即使我們沒有生來就有的天賦，也應該要努力提升自己，而不是在意天資如何。抱怨自己不聰明或是沒有天分，只是給自己偷懶的藉口。以數學為例，在小學時，很多人會因為跟不上課堂的進度而被貼上「數學不好」的標籤。但實際上，每個人都有數學能力的潛能。許多研究表明，人人都有「數學腦」，數學能力是可以透過學習和練習來獲得的。而這種成長心態也適用於發展其他的能力。很讓人興奮吧？

inborn talent 天賦　innate 生來就有的
numerous 許多的　acquire 獲得、習得

Self-Care 自我關懷

Accept Yourself, Warts and All.

Self-acceptance is like giving yourself a big hug, recognizing that you're awesome just the way you are. It's about loving and embracing every part of you, even the warts, the bits you're not so happy about. Here's a simple idea to practice self-acceptance: every day, stand in front of the mirror and say one thing you like about yourself. It could be anything—maybe your sense of humor or how you helped a friend. For instance, if you did a good job in completing your homework or just made a killer omelet, acknowledge it. Say, "Hey, I did that, and I did it really well." This is like giving yourself a pat on the back regularly. It boosts your confidence and helps you see yourself in a positive light. Remember, the more you appreciate yourself, the brighter your world becomes.

接受自己的缺點和一切

接受自己就像是給你自己一個大大的擁抱，認可自己本來就很棒。這是在講愛自己和擁抱自己的每一個部分，即使是那些你不太高興的缺點，也要接受。有一個練習接納自我的簡單方法：每天站在鏡子前，說一件你喜歡自己的事。它可以是任何的事情 —— 也許是你的幽默感，或你怎麼幫助了一個朋友。例如：你完成了一份讓你滿意的作業，或是剛煎了一個漂亮的蛋捲，認可它，說：「嘿，我做到了，而且做得很好。」這就像是定期地給自己拍拍背一樣（肯定自己）。這會增強你的自信，幫助你用正面的眼光看待自己。記住，你越欣賞自己，你的世界就越明亮。

killer 漂亮的、厲害無比的　acknowledge 認可
a pat on the back 拍拍背 （肯定自己）

213

Day 90

Philosophy 人生觀

Forgiveness Is for You.

There's this idea that time can heal everything, and in a way, it's true. When someone does something that hurts us, we might feel really upset at first. But as time passes, we sometimes find those hard feelings fading away. Yet, holding onto anger and resentment doesn't change what happened; it only makes it harder to forgive. Research shows these feelings can even mess with your health, like harming the immune system and triggering emotional gastrointestinal diseases, among other issues. So, what's the point in keeping them around? Here's a thought: try forgiving everyone for everything, and do it now, not years later. It sounds tough, I know, but it's really for you, not them. Forgiving is like setting yourself free from carrying around all that heavy stuff. It's not about saying what they did was okay. It's about giving yourself the gift of moving on and finding happiness. When you let go of grudges, you make room for peace in your heart. And that's a pretty amazing feeling.

原諒是為了自己

有一個觀念，認為時間能治癒一切，從某種程度來說，這是對的。當有人做了傷害我們的事，一開始我們可能會感到非常難過。但隨著時間的流逝，我們有時會發現那些痛苦的感覺逐漸消失。然而，抱著憤怒和怨恨並不能改變過去所發生的事，這只會讓你更難原諒。研究證明，這些情緒甚至會影響我們的健康，例如損害免疫系統和引發情緒性的胃腸疾病等問題。那麼，留著這些情緒又有什麼意義呢？這裡有個想法：試著現在就原諒所有人、所有事，而不是等到多年以後。我知道這聽起來很困難，但這真的是為了你，不是為了他們。原諒就像是讓自己從背負著沉重的包袱中解脫。這並不是說他們做的事情是情有可原的，而是給自己一個繼續前進和找到快樂的禮物。當你放下怨恨時，你的心就會騰出祥和的空間，這是很好的感覺。

214

fade 逐漸消失　immune system 免疫系統
trigger 引發　grudge 怨恨

215

Phase
10

. . . .

Continually Go Beyond

持續超越

"So, in the face of difficulties, remember,
it's not about the strength of your punch but the spirit that drives it."

-from Day 96-

「所以，當面對困難時，
記住，重要的不是你拳頭的力量，
而是驅動你持續出拳的精神。」

Gratitude 感恩

Gratitude Journaling for a Better Tomorrow.

Let me ask you a question: have you ever thought about starting a gratitude journal? It's a simple but powerful way to shift your focus and boost your mood. All you need to do is write down between three and five things you're thankful for each day. They can be big or small—from a beautiful sunset to a tasty snack or a nice message from a friend. Taking the time to reflect on the positive aspects of your life can really change your perspective and make you feel happier overall. It's like training your mind to look for the good stuff, and if you really think about it, there's always something good to be found. Do this exercise before going to bed every night, and your subconscious mind will keep thinking about how great your life is. Then, you'll have a much better day the next day. Give it a try and see how it makes a difference in your life!

用感恩日記迎接更好的明天

讓我問你一個問題：你有沒有想過開始寫感恩日記？這是個簡單又有用的方法，可以轉移注意力並改善你的心情。你只需要每天寫下三到五件讓你感激的事情。無論大小──從美麗的日落到美味的點心，或是朋友傳來的暖心訊息。花點時間想想你生活裡的正面事物，可以真的改變你看事情的角度，讓你整體的感覺更快樂。這就像在訓練你的大腦去尋找美好的事物，如果你真的有去想，總會找到一些好東西。每天晚上睡覺前做這個練習，你的潛意識將會不斷地去想你的生活有多麼美好。這樣，到了隔天你將會有更美好的一天。試試看，看它是怎麼改變你的生活！

boost 改善、提高　reflect on 思考、考慮
aspect 方面、層面　subconscious mind 潛意識

Day 92

Conquering Adversity 克服逆境

Focus on What You Can Control.

Many things in life are completely out of your hands. Focus on what you can control. It's like steering your own ship in the ocean of life. It's putting your energy where it really counts and can make a difference, instead of worrying about the waves you can't calm. Try this: make a list of things that worry you and divide them into two categories—things you can control and things you can't. For example, you can't control the traffic on an important day, but you can control how early you leave. Likewise, you can't control the outcome in the university admissions process, but you can control the amount of effort you make before applying to college. Whenever you find yourself anxious because of stress, look at your list and ask, "Is this something I can change?" If yes, work on it; if not, let it be. This helps you focus on the actions that truly matter and teaches you to let go of unnecessary worries. Remember, where focus goes, energy flows. Keep steering your ship wisely!

專注在你所能控制的事

生活中有許多事情是完全不在你的控制範圍內。專注於你能控制的事物，就像在人生的海洋上駕駛自己的船。它是你投入精力真正重要的地方並能帶來改變，而不是擔心你所無法平息的海浪。試著這麼做：列出讓你感到擔憂的事情，並將它們分為兩類──你能控制的事和不能控制的事。例如，你無法控制重要日子裡的交通情形，但可以控制自己多早出發。同樣，你無法控制大學申請的結果，但可以控制自己在申請大學之前所做的努力。每當你因為壓力而感到焦慮時，看看清單並問自己：「這是不是我可以改變的事？」如果是，那就著手去改；如果不是，那就順其自然吧。這樣可以幫助你專注於真正重要的行動，並教會你放下不必要的擔憂。記住，你的專注在哪裡，你的精力就用在哪裡。繼續明智地駕駛你的船吧！

out of your hands 不在你的控制範圍內
steer 駕駛　category 種類、類別　outcome 結果

Learning 學習

It Takes Just 15 Minutes.

All you can do is all you can do, but trust me, all you can do is enough. If you're already giving it your all, don't beat yourself up for not doing more. If, however, you find yourself slacking off, take action now. Even something as simple as setting a timer for 15 minutes (or 10, or even 5) can make a world of difference. As long as it feels manageable, go for it. Here's an idea: spend 15 minutes, right now if possible, either copying or reading out the passages in this book. If you haven't started doing it yet, it'll be a small step that will kickstart your learning again. And if you're up for it, increase the time by another 15 minutes, and keep doing that until you need to take a break. The key is consistency. Use this 15-minute technique daily, and before you know it, you'll be back on track with your learning journey.

只要 15 分鐘

你所能做的就是你所能做的,但相信我,你所能做的已經足夠。如果你已經全力以赴,就不要為自己不能做更多而自責。然而,如果你發現自己懈怠了,現在就採取行動。即使是簡單的設定計時器 15 分鐘(或 10 分鐘、甚至 5 分鐘)也能帶來巨大的改變。只要覺得做得到,就去做吧。我有個建議:如果現在可以的話,花 15 分鐘,抄寫或唸出這本書裡的文章。如果你還沒有開始這樣做,這將是你重新啟動學習的一小步。如果你願意,可以再加 15 分鐘,持續這樣做,直到你想休息為止。關鍵是持之以恆。每天使用這個 15 分鐘的技巧,不知不覺,你已經回到了學習之旅的正軌上。

slack off 懈怠、偷懶　manageable 做得到的、行得通的
consistency 持之以恆

Day 94

Goals & Dreams 目標與夢想

The Past Doesn't Have to Equal the Future.

I've got some great news! Your past doesn't have to define your future, not one bit. Yeah, you might have messed up before, but guess what? Most of the super successful people you hear about started with nothing. They were not born rich—they earned it. And most of them messed up lots before they hit it big. Don't be fooled into thinking they just got lucky; they worked really hard for years to achieve what they now have. So, don't get stuck on past results (like poor grades, going to a poorly ranked college, being in a low position at work, etc.) thinking that's all you can do. Your future potential is limitless. So, aim high, aim for what you really want, not just what you think you can get based on your past. Trust me, you'll be glad you did.

過去不必等於未來

我有好消息！你的過往完全沒有必要去限制你的未來。是的，你也許之前搞砸了，但你知道嗎？你聽過的大多數很成功的人士當初都是白手起家。他們不是生來就富有 —— 他們是賺來的。而且，他們在成功之前也搞砸了許多事情。不要傻傻以為他們只是運氣好，他們可是努力奮鬥了很多年才有今天。所以，你不要擺脫不了過去的結果（像是成績爛、學校差、職位低……），誤以為那就是你的極限。你未來的潛力是無窮的。所以，目標要高遠，追求你真正想要的東西，而且不只是你覺得你過去可以達到的範圍。相信我，你將會很高興自己有這麼做。

define 界定、限定　not one bit 完全、一點也不
be fooled （傻傻的）被騙

225

Love 愛

Every Day Beats Special Days.

We often think of romance as special days of celebration and special dates. We think that the perfect confession, the perfect proposal, or the perfect wedding day are the most important parts of a relationship. But guess what? As important as these special days are, they are nowhere near as important as the daily kindnesses that you show each other. If you are kind to each other all the time, every day can be as sweet as your honeymoon. Right now, think about several things that you could do to make your relationship a little bit more special. Perhaps, you could send a romantic text to your other half, give them a drink they like without being asked, or buy them something small but unexpected. It really doesn't have to be a big thing. Remember, much of the time, it's the thought that counts, not the expense.

小日子勝過大日子

我們經常將浪漫視為在特殊節日的慶祝或有個特別的約會,認為完美的告白、完美的求婚或完美的婚禮,是感情關係中最重要的部分。但猜猜怎麼了?固然那些特殊的日子很重要,但那些卻遠不如你們每天對彼此展現的善意那麼重要。如果你們總是善待彼此,那麼每一天都會像蜜月一樣甜蜜。現在,想想幾件你可以做的事情,讓你們的關係變得更加特別。也許,你可以傳個浪漫的訊息給你的另一半,主動給他們一杯他們喜愛的飲品,或是出乎意料的買個小東西送給他們。這真的不用是多大的事。記住,很多時候,重要的是你的心意,而不是花費了多少。

confession 告白　proposal 求婚
nowhere near 遠不如、遠遠不及　expense 花費

Grit 恆毅力

The Spirit to Keep Punching.

Grit is like being in a boxing ring with life. It's not always about how hard you can hit, but how many hits you can take and keep moving forward. It's about not letting a knockdown turn into a knockout. Every challenge you face is going to throw punches at you. Some will be soft, easy to dodge, while others might hit hard, knocking you down. But having grit means even if you get knocked down, you never stay down. You keep punching, not because you're unafraid or unharmed, but because you're determined. You know that with each punch you throw back, you're one step closer to winning your fight, achieving your goals. So, in the face of difficulties, remember, it's not about the strength of your punch but the spirit that drives it. Keep punching, keep moving, and you'll see, nothing can keep you down for long.

持續出拳的精神

恆毅力就像你在拳擊擂台上與自己的人生單挑。重點不在你能打出多重的出拳，而在你能承受多少次的挨打，並繼續向前。這是為了不讓一次的被打倒變成終結性的出局。你面對的每一個挑戰都會朝你揮拳，有些是輕擊，容易閃避；而有些可能是重擊，將你打倒。然而擁有恆毅力，這意味著即使你被打倒，你也絕不會永遠爬不起來。你會持續出拳，不是因為不害怕或沒有受傷，而是因為有決心。你知道你反擊回去的每一拳，都讓你離贏得勝利、實現目標更近一步。所以，當面對困難時，記住，重要的不是拳頭的力量，而是驅動你持續出拳的精神。繼續出拳，持續前進，會發現沒有什麼能讓你永遠倒下。

boxing ring 拳擊擂台　knockdown （被）打倒
knockout 終結性的出局 （KO）　dodge 閃避、躲過

Day 97

Happiness 快樂

The Fewer Rules You Have, the Happier You'll Be.

You know how we sometimes trap ourselves with lots of "I don't likes" and "I can't accepts"? Things like, "I don't like this," "I can't accept that," or insisting "It has to be this way." The more we do this, the more the world seems to fight back, and it can make us feel pretty down. But here's a cool tip: try to start letting go of these self-imposed rules. For instance, if you believe people must answer you in a certain way, you need to understand that they might have different rules and that you can't really force others to follow your rules. Then, let go of the rule and be willing to accept people as they really are. You might be surprised! When you start accepting things you thought you couldn't, life gets simpler. Open your heart and drop those stubborn views. The fewer rules you set for yourself and others, the happier you'll be.

規則越少，心越快樂

你有沒有發現我們有時會用很多的「我不喜歡」和「我不能接受」來限制自己？像是「我不喜歡這個」、「我不能接受那個」，或是堅持「這一定要這樣做（或事情必須是這樣的）」。我們越是這樣，世界似乎越是反抗，這樣會讓我們很不快樂。不過有個好建議：試著開始放下這些自己強加的規則。例如，如果你認為大家必須用某種方式來回應你，你需要理解他們可能有不同的規則，而你不能真的強迫別人遵循你的規則。然後，放下規則，願意接受人們都是這個樣子。你可能會感到驚喜！當你開始接受自己原本認為不能接受的事物時，生活會變得更簡單。敞開你的心胸，放下那些執念。你為自己和他人設下的規則越少，你就會越快樂。

trap 限制 （讓自己被困住）   self-imposed rule 自己強加的規則
stubborn 固執的、執著的

231

Growth 成長

You're Going to Go off Course.

Here's a fun fact: when you're on a plane, you're actually off course about 95% of the time! Crazy, right? But the pilot keeps adjusting, and, like magic, you arrive at your destination. The same goes for life. You're going to go off course; that's a given. Don't try to never mess up or even avoid the same mistakes forever. No one's that perfect! What's important is catching those mistakes and learning how to get back on target. The name of the game is reducing how often you go off track, not beating yourself up when you do. So, if you find yourself going the wrong way, just remember it's all part of the journey. Course correct, keep moving, and you'll still reach your destination.

你一定有走偏的時候

一個有趣的事實：當你坐飛機時，實際上大約有 95% 的時間都是偏離航線的！很瘋狂，對吧？然而飛行員會不斷地做調整，就像變魔術一樣，你會到達目的地。人生也不例外。你一定會有走偏的時候，這是不可避免的。不要拘泥在永不犯錯，甚至是永不貳過。沒有人是那麼完美的！重要的是，當你意識到錯誤時，要學著如何重新回到正軌。重點在於減少你偏離軌道的次數，而不在於犯錯時過於自責。因此，如果你發現自己走錯了路，請記住：這都是旅程的一部分。立即修正航線，繼續前進，你終究會到達目的地的。

off course 偏離路線的　back on target 回到正軌的
go off track 走錯路

Day 99

Self-Care 自我關懷

The Art of Doing Nothing.

Did you know it's actually fine to just do nothing once in a while? If you think taking a break is only for lazy people, it's time to change that mindset. Like breathing, there's a rhythm to work and relaxation—inhale is work, exhale is rest, and both are super important. Constantly working without a break is like holding your breath for too long—eventually, you have to breathe out. Pushing yourself non-stop can lead to burnout or even getting sick. Your body's telling you, "I need some downtime." So, if you want to relax and watch part of a TV series, go for a stroll, get a really good night's sleep, or even take a few days off, that's totally okay. It's your way of exhaling. But remember, balance is key. It's not about doing nothing or being busy all the time, but about finding the right mix of activity and relaxation, say 70% work and 30% relaxation. Stay balanced, and you'll feel so much better!

什麼都不做的藝術

你知道嗎？偶爾什麼事都不做其實是很好的。如果你認為休息只是懶人的專利，那麼是時候改變這種想法了。就像呼吸一樣，工作和放鬆之間也有節奏——吸氣是工作，吐氣是休息，兩者都非常重要。不停歇地工作就像憋氣太久——最終，你必須吐氣。不停地強迫自己可能會精疲力盡或甚至生病。你的身體在告訴你：「我需要一些休息。」所以，如果你想放鬆一下，看個影集、散步、睡個好覺，甚至休息幾天，那都可以。這是你吐氣的方式。但記住，平衡是關鍵。不是要你什麼都不做或一直忙不停，而是找到工作和放鬆的最佳比例，例如 70% 的工作和 30% 的放鬆。保持平衡，你會感覺好多了！

rhythm 節奏　eventually 最終地　burnout 精疲力盡
downtime 休息　stroll 散步

Philosophy 人生觀

It's Never Too Late.

Did you know that it's never too late to pick up something new or make a change? Well, it's a little-known truth. Life's flexible. Suppose you've been thinking about getting fit but feel like you've missed the boat. Not at all! You can start small. For example, try a 10-minute home workout, take a brisk walk around your neighborhood, or even join a beginner's Pilates class. These little steps can kickstart your fitness journey. It's all about taking that first step and enjoying the process. Every small effort counts and adds up to big changes over time. The same goes for any new skill or hobby. Want to learn cooking? Start with simple recipes. Dreaming of painting? Begin with basic techniques. It's your journey, and it's never too late to embark on it. Dive in, explore, and most importantly, have fun with it. You've got this!

永遠不會太晚

你知道嗎？學習新事物或做出改變永遠不嫌晚，然而卻少有人知道。人生是充滿彈性的。假設你一直想要開始健身，但感覺自己好像錯過了最佳時機。其實一點也不！你可以從簡單的開始做起。例如，嘗試做一個 10 分鐘的居家運動，或在住家附近快走，甚至加入一個初學者的皮拉提斯課程。這些小步驟可以啟動你的健身之旅。重要的是踏出第一步並享受過程。每一點小努力都會隨著時間累積而成為重大的改變，對於任何新技能或興趣也是如此。想學習烹飪嗎？從簡單的食譜開始。夢想著繪畫嗎？那就從基礎技巧開始。這是你的旅程，開始永遠不會太晚。全心投入、去探索，並且最重要的是，要享受其中。你做得到！

workout 運動　recipe 食譜
embark on 開始（通常用於旅程）

Eurasian Publishing Group
圓神出版事業機構
用心與你對話・網野無限實廣

如何出版社
Solutions Publishing

www.booklife.com.tw

reader@mail.eurasian.com.tw

Happy Language 166

抄寫英語的奇蹟：1天10分鐘，英語和人生都起飛

作　　者／林熙 Brett Lindsay
發 行 人／簡志忠
出 版 者／如何出版社有限公司
地　　址／臺北市南京東路四段50號6樓之1
電　　話／（02）2579-6600・2579-8800・2570-3939
傳　　真／（02）2579-0338・2577-3220・2570-3636
副 社 長／陳秋月
副總編輯／賴良珠
專案企畫／尉遲佩文
責任編輯／柳怡如
校　　對／柳怡如・歐玟秀
美術編輯／林韋伶
行銷企畫／陳禹伶・林雅雯
印務統籌／劉鳳剛・高榮祥
監　　印／高榮祥
排　　版／莊寶鈴
經 銷 商／叩應股份有限公司
郵撥帳號／18707239
法律顧問／圓神出版事業機構法律顧問　蕭雄淋律師
印　　刷／國碩印前科技股份有限公司
2024 年 3 月　初版
2024 年 9 月　17 刷

定價 380 元　　　ISBN 978-986-136-683-8

俗話說：「要怎麼吃掉一頭大象呢？」答案是：「一口一口地吃。」
你有一個大目標嗎？太棒了！把它切成你可以應付的小塊，這些小塊
就是你的里程碑。

——《抄寫英語的奇蹟》

◆ **很喜歡這本書，很想要分享**

圓神書活網線上提供團購優惠，
或洽讀者服務部 02-2579-6600。

◆ **美好生活的提案家，期待為您服務**

圓神書活網 www.Booklife.com.tw
非會員歡迎體驗優惠，會員獨享累計福利！

國家圖書館出版品預行編目資料

抄寫英語的奇蹟：1天10分鐘，英語和人生都起飛 / 林熙（Brett Lindsay）著.
-- 初版. -- 臺北市：如何出版社有限公司, 2024.03
　　240 面；17×23公分 --（Happy language；166）

　　ISBN 978-986-136-683-8（平裝）
　　1.CST：英語　2.CST：讀本
805.18　　　　　　　　　　　　　　　　　　　　　113000382